Anne of Green Gables

清秀佳人

Original Author   Lucy Maud Montgomery
Adaptor   Brian J. Stuart
Illustrator   An Ji-Yeon

WORDS
450

U0070029

MP3

Let's Enjoy Masterpieces!

All the beautiful fairy tales and masterpieces that you have encountered during your childhood remain as warm memories in your adulthood. This time, let's indulge in the world of masterpieces through English. You can enjoy the depth and beauty of original works, which you can't enjoy through Chinese translations.

The stories are easy for you to understand because of your familiarity with them. When you enjoy reading, your ability to understand English will also rapidly improve.

This series of *Let's Enjoy Masterpieces* is a special reading comprehension booster program, devised to improve reading comprehension for beginners whose command of English is not satisfactory, or who are elementary, middle, and high school students. With this program, you can enjoy reading masterpieces in English with fun and efficiency.

This carefully planned program is composed of 5 levels, from the beginner level of 350 words to the intermediate and advanced levels of 1,000 words. With this program's level-by-level system, you are able to read famous texts in English and to savor the true pleasure of the world's language.

The program is well conceived, composed of reader-friendly explanations of English expressions and grammar, quizzes to help the student learn vocabulary and understand the meaning of the texts, and fabulous illustrations that adorn every page. In addition, with our "Guide to Listening," not only is reading comprehension enhanced but also listening comprehension skills are highlighted.

In the audio recording of the book, texts are vividly read by professional American actors. The texts are rewritten, according to the levels of the readers by an expert editorial staff of native speakers, on the basis of standard American English with the ministry of education recommended vocabulary. Therefore, it will be of great help even for all the students that want to learn English.

Please indulge yourself in the fun of reading and listening to English through *Let's Enjoy Masterpieces*.

露西・莫德・ 蒙哥馬利

Lucy Maud Montgomery
(1874–1942)

Lucy Maud Montgomery was a Canadian female writer. She was born on a small island called Prince Edward Island in November 1874. As a girl, she began to enjoy writing.

In 1904, reading through her journals that she wrote a long time ago, she came across this note:

"Elderly couple applies to orphan asylum for a boy to help with the farm chores. By mistake, a girl is sent to them."

This fired her imagination and inspired the creation of Anne.

In 1905, *Anne of Green Gables* was finished. Throughout the ten books in the Anne series, Montgomery remained a writer at heart, who always found her writing materials close at hand and whose beautiful descriptions of scenery, warm-heartedness, and sadness stand out.

Anne of Green Gables takes place on a farm, in the quiet town of Avonlea, Canada. Matthew and Marilla, unmarried siblings, live on the farm. They decide to adopt an orphan boy to help them handle the farm work; however, the orphanage sent a talkative girl instead.

As this girl, Anne Shirley, begins to live with Matthew and Marilla in the house with a green roof, not a day goes by without some funny episodes. Anne devotes herself to her studies as a result of a rivalry with Gilbert Blythe, one of her classmates, who taunts her for her red hair, which she is extremely sensitive about.

Finally, Anne succeeds in attending a prestigious university; however, she gives up her aspirations for a four-year degree, as Marilla's health deteriorates after Matthew's death. Gilbert hears of her decision and gives up his post as the teacher at Avonlea School so that Anne can teach there. Finally, Gilbert and Anne reconcile with each other.

Since its publication in 1908, the Anne series has been loved all around the world.

HOW TO USE THIS BOOK
本書使用說明

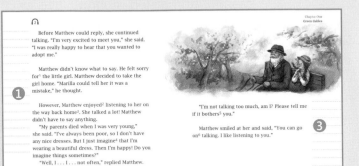

① Original English texts

It is easy to understand the meaning of the text, because the text is rewritten according to the levels of the readers.

② Explanation of the vocabulary

The words and expressions that include vocabulary above the elementary level are clearly defined.

③ Response notes

Spaces are included in the book so you can take notes about what you don't understand or what you want to remember.

④ One point lesson

In-depth analyses of major grammar points and expressions help you to understand sentences with difficult grammar.

🎧 Audio Recording

In the audio recording, native speakers narrate the texts in standard American English. By combining the written words and the audio recording, you can listen to English with great ease.

Audio books have been popular in Britain and America for many decades. They allow the listener to experience the proper word pronunciation and sentence intonation that add important meaning and drama to spoken English. Students will benefit from listening to the recording twenty or more times.

After you are familiar with the text and recording, listen once more with your eyes closed to check your listening comprehension. Finally, after you can listen with your eyes closed and understand every word and every sentence, you are then ready to mimic the native speaker.

Then you should make a recording by reading the text yourself. Then play both recordings to compare your oral skills with those of a native speaker.

HOW TO IMPROVE READING ABILITY

如何增進英文閱讀能力

① *Catch key words*

Read the key words in the sentences and practice catching the gist of the meaning of the sentence. You might question how working with a few important words could enhance your reading ability. However, it's quite effective. If you continue to use this method, you will find out that the key words and your knowledge of people and situations enables you to understand the sentence.

② *Divide long sentences*

Read in chunks of meaning, dividing sentences into meaningful chunks of information. In the book, chunks are arranged in sentences according to meaning. If you consider the sentences backwards or grammatically, your reading speed will be slow and you will find it difficult to listen to English.

You are ready to move to a more sophisticated level of comprehension when you find that narrowly focusing on chunks is irritating. Instead of considering the chunks, you will make it a habit to read the sentence from the beginning to the end to figure out the meaning of the whole.

③ Make inferences and assumptions

Making inferences and assumptions is part of your ability. If you don't know, try to guess the meaning of the words. Although you don't know all the words in context, don't go straight to the dictionary. Developing an ability to make inferences in the context is important.

The first way to figure out the meaning of a word is from its context. If you cannot make head or tail out of the meaning of a word, look at what comes before or after it. Ask yourself what can happen in such a situation. Make your best guess as to the word's meaning. Then check the explanations of the word in the book or look up the word in a dictionary.

④ Read a lot and reread the same book many times

There is no shortcut to mastering English. Only if you do a lot of reading will you make your way to the summit. Read fun and easy books with an average of less than one new word per page. Try to immerse yourself in English as often as you can.

Spend time "swimming" in English. Language learning research has shown that immersing yourself in English will help you improve your English, even though you may not be aware of what you're learning.

CONTENTS

Introduction 4

How to Use This Book 6

How to Improve Reading Ability 8

Before You Read 12

Chapter One

Green Gables 14

    Comprehension Quiz 24

Chapter Two

I Love It Here. 26

    Comprehension Quiz 38

Chapter Three

I Hate You, Gilbert. 40

    Comprehension Quiz 50

Before You Read 52

Chapter Four

Anne's Mistakes 54
Comprehension Quiz 66

Chapter Five

You Did It! 68
Comprehension Quiz 78

Chapter Six

Matthew and Marilla 80
Comprehension Quiz 92

Appendixes

❶ Basic Grammar 94
❷ Guide to Listening Comprehension 98
❸ Listening Guide 102
❹ Listening Comprehension 106

Translation 110
Answers 130

Before You Read

train
火車

Train Station
火車站

platform
月臺

railroad
鐵路

arrive leave
抵達   離開

Has the five-thirty train arrived yet?
5點30分的火車到了嗎？

stationmaster
站長

boat
小船

get on the boat
上船

get out of the boat
從船裡出來

play in the field
在田野玩

woods
森林

reds and yellows of the trees
紅紅黃黃的樹木

wedding ceremony
結婚典禮

bride **bridegroom**
新娘   新郎

wife **husband**
妻子   丈夫

graveyard
墓地

river
河

church
教堂

go to church on Sundays
星期天去做禮拜

I can imagine her in church
with her white dress.
我能想像她在教堂穿上白紗的樣子。

vicar
教區牧師

farmer
農夫

work on the farm
在農場上工作

farmhouse
農舍

12

The Town of Avonlea
艾凡利鎮

bridge
橋

blackboard
黑板

teacher
老師

town center
城鎮中心

school **late for school**
學校 上學遲到

bank
銀行

Anne and some friends stayed late at school.
安妮和一些朋友在學校待得很晚。

driveway / road
車道 / 馬路

The river will carry the boat
down to the bridge.
河流會使小船順流而下到橋邊。

farm
農場

doctor's
醫院

orchard
果園

lane
小路

garden
庭院

field Anne loved everything in Avonlea.
田野 安妮喜愛艾凡利的每樣事物。

Chapter One

🎧1 # Green Gables

Matthew Cuthbert was an old man, almost sixty years old. He and his sister, Marilla, lived at Green Gables. It was a small farm near the town of Avonlea.

On this day, Matthew was wearing his best clothes. He was excited[1]. It was a special day. He drove[2] to the train station[3] in Avonlea.

"Has the five-thirty train arrived yet[4]?" Matthew asked the stationmaster[5].

"Yes, it has," replied the stationmaster. "And a little girl is waiting for you now, over there[6]."

1. **excited** [ɪk`saɪtɪd] (a.) 興奮的
2. **drive** [draɪv] (v.) 駕車 (drive-drove-driven)
3. **train station** 火車站
4. **yet** [jet] (adv.) （用於疑問句）現在已經
5. **stationmaster** [`steɪʃən,mæstər] (n.) 站長
6. **over there** 在那裡
7. **expect** [ɪk`spekt] (v.) 期待
8. **adopt** [ə`dɑːpt] (v.) 收養
9. **orphanage** [`ɔːrfənɪdʒ] (n.) 孤兒院
10. **thin** [θɪn] (a.) 瘦的；細的

Matthew was shocked.
"A little girl? But we were expecting[7] a boy!"

Matthew and Marilla had decided to adopt[8] a boy from an orphanage[9]. Matthew wanted someone to help him on the farm.

Matthew saw a thin[10] girl with red hair. She saw Matthew looking at her, and ran to him.
"Are you Mr. Cuthbert of Green Gables?"

One Point Lesson

◆ **Has** the five-thirty train **arrived** yet?
  5 點 30 分的火車到了嗎？

現在完成式：用 has（單數）或 have（複數）作為助動詞，
　　　　　　構成現在完成式。意即，現在完成式是：
　　　　　　「助動詞 have/has ＋動詞的過去分詞」。

e.g. I **have** just **finished** it. 我剛做完這件事。
　　 I **have lost** my book. 我掉了書。

Before Matthew could reply, she continued talking. "I'm very excited to meet you," she said. "I was really happy to hear that you wanted to adopt me."

Matthew didn't know what to say. He felt sorry for[1] the little girl. Matthew decided to take the girl home. "Marilla could tell her it was a mistake," he thought.

However, Matthew enjoyed[2] listening to her on the way back home[3]. She talked a lot! Matthew didn't have to say anything.

"My parents died when I was very young," she said. "I've always been poor, so I don't have any nice dresses. But I just imagine[4] that I'm wearing a beautiful dress. Then I'm happy! Do you imagine things sometimes?"

"Well, I . . . I . . . not often," replied Matthew.

1. **feel sorry for**
   對……感到抱歉
2. **enjoy** [ɪn`dʒɔɪ] (v.)
   享受（後接 V-ing）
3. **on the way back home**
   在回家的路上
4. **imagine** [ɪ`mædʒɪn] (v.) 想像
5. **bother** [`bɑːðər] (v.)
   煩擾；使惱怒
6. **go on** 繼續（後接 V-ing）

"I'm not talking too much, am I? Please tell me if it bothers[5] you."

Matthew smiled at her and said, "You can go on[6] talking. I like listening to you."

🔹 **I've** (have) always **been** poor. 我一直很窮。

be 的過去分詞為 been。

I've been here for a week.
我在這裡已經一星期了。

When they arrived at[1] Green Gables, Marilla came to the door to greet[2] them. She was smiling and her arms were open. But when she saw the little girl, she suddenly[3] stopped.

"Matthew, who's this?" asked Marilla. "Where's the boy?"

Matthew sighed[4]. "The orphanage made a mistake[5]. They sent a girl instead of[6] a boy."

The child was listening carefully[7]. Suddenly she started to cry. "Oh, you don't want me!" she cried. "Now you'll send me back[8]!"

---

1. **arrive at** 到達；抵達
2. **greet** [griːt] (v.) 迎接
3. **suddenly** [ˋsʌdnli] (adv.) 突然地
4. **sigh** [saɪ] (v.) 嘆氣

5. **make a mistake** 犯錯
6. **instead of** 而不是……
7. **carefully** [ˋkeərfəli] (adv.) 仔細地
8. **send back** 送回去

"Oh, now, now," said Marilla as she put an arm on[9] the girl's shoulders. "Don't cry."

"Oh, this is just the worst[10] thing in my life[11]!" the girl cried out.

Marilla felt sorry for the girl. "Well, you can stay here just for tonight," she said.

---

9. put *A* on *B* 把 A 放在 B 上面
10. **worst** [wɜːst] (a.) 最壞的   11. **in one's life** 一生中

"Now, what's your name?" The girl stopped crying.

"Would you[1] please call[2] me 'Cordelia'?" she asked.

"Cordelia? Is that your name?"

"No, it isn't, but it's a very beautiful name, don't you think?" said the girl. "I like to imagine that my name is Cordelia, because my real[3] name, Anne Shirley, is not very nice.

Marilla shook[4] her head[5]. "This girl has too much imagination[6]," she thought.

1. **Would you . . . ?**
   你可以⋯⋯嗎？；請你⋯⋯
2. **call** *A B* 把 A 稱為 B
3. **real** [rɪəl] (a.) 真實的

4. **shake** [ʃeɪk] (v.) 搖動
   (shake-shook-shaken)
5. **shake one's head** 搖頭
6. **imagination**
   [ɪˌmædʒəˈneɪʃən] (n.) 想像力

When the girl was in bed, Marilla spoke to Matthew. "She must go back[7] to the orphanage tomorrow."

Matthew coughed[8] a little.

"Marilla, don't you think . . ." he stopped. "She's a nice little thing[9], you know."

"Matthew Cuthbert!" said Marilla. She only called[10] him by their last name[11] when she was angry. "Are you telling me that you want to keep[12] her?"

7. **go back** 回去
8. **cough** [kɒːf] (v.) 咳嗽
9. **thing** [θɪŋ] (n.)
   人；東西（口語化的說法）
10. **call** *A* **by** *B* 以B來稱呼A
11. **last name** 姓
    （first name：名）
12. **keep** [kiːp] (v.) 撫養

Matthew was uncomfortable[1], and a little nervous[2].

"Well, she's clever[3], and interesting, and . . ."

"But we don't need a girl!" said Marilla. "She'll be hard to[4] take care of[5], and not much help to us."

"Perhaps she needs us," Matthew replied. "Look, Marilla, she's had an unhappy life. She can help you in the house. I can get a boy from the village to help me on the farm. What do you think?"

Marilla thought for a long time. She did feel sorry for the girl. Finally, she said, "All right. I agree. The poor child can stay. I'll look after[6] her."

1. **uncomfortable** [ʌnˈkʌmfərtəbəl] (a.) 不舒服的
2. **nervous** [ˈnɜːrvəs] (a.) 緊張的
3. **clever** [ˈklevər] (a.) 聰明的
4. **be hard to . . .** 很困難
5. **take care of** 照顧；處理
6. **look after** 照顧

Matthew smiled. "Be kind to her, Marilla.
I think she needs a lot of love."

One Point Lesson

♦ She **did** feel sorry for the girl. 他對這女孩感到很抱歉。

強調語氣：do 可當助詞，放在原形動詞前面，形成強調句。

e.g. I **do** like my teacher. 我喜歡我的老師。

A Fill in the blanks.

thin   imagination   red

❶ She was small and _____.

❷ She had _____ hair.

❸ She had a lot of _____.

B True or False.

T F ❶ Green Gables was the name of a small town near Avonlea.

T F ❷ Matthew and Marilla wanted a boy to help them on the farm.

T F ❸ Anne's parents died when she was very young.

T F ❹ Anne's real name was Cordelia Shirley.

C Fill in the blanks according to the example.

> Marilla *felt* sorry for Anne.
>
> ⇨ Marilla *did feel* sorry for Anne.

❶ He wanted to meet the child.

> ⇨ He _____ to meet the child.

❷ She likes to imagine things.

> ⇨ She _____ to imagine things.

D Fill in the blanks with the given words.

> make   enjoy   send   adopt   decide

Matthew and Marilla wanted to **❶**_____ a boy, but the people at the orphanage **❷**_____ a mistake. They **❸**_____ a girl to the Cuthberts instead of a boy. However, Matthew **❹** _____ listening to Anne. Finally, they **❺** _____ to keep Anne.

Chapter Two

🎧 I Love It Here.

The next morning at breakfast, Marilla said, "Well, Anne, we have decided to adopt you. Anne started to cry.

"Why, child, what's the matter[1]?" asked Marilla.
"I'm crying," said Anne, "because I'm so happy! I love it here! Oh, thank you, thank you!"

"Now stop crying, child," said Marilla. She was a bit[2] upset[3] because Anne was crying.

Anne stopped crying, and said, "Can I call you Aunt[4] Marilla? I've never had any family at all[5], so I'd really like to[6] have a nice and kind aunt. We could imagine you're my mother's sister."

Marilla was surprised[7]. "I couldn't do that," answered Marilla firmly[8]. Now Anne was surprised.

"Don't you ever[9] imagine things?" she asked.
"No, I don't have time for[10] that," Marilla said. "I do the housework[11] and look after Matthew. There's no time in this house to imagine things."

1. **matter** [ˈmætər] (n.) 事情；問題
2. **a bit** 有一點
3. **upset** [ʌpˈset] (a.) 苦惱的
4. **aunt** [ænt] (n.) 姑姑；阿姨
5. **at all** 絲毫
6. **I'd like to** 我想要……
7. **be surprised** 驚訝
8. **firmly** [ˈfɜːrmli] (adv.) 堅決地
9. **ever** [ˈevər] (adv.) 曾經
10. **have time for** 有時間做……
11. **housework** [ˈhaʊswɜːrk] (n.) 家事

One Point Lesson

◆ **I've never had** any family at all. 我從來都沒有任何家人。

have + never/ever + 動詞的過去分詞：從來沒有／曾經有。
現在完成式，表示從未或曾經做過什麼。

e.g. **I've never been** to U.S. 我從未去過美國。

Anne was quiet for a short time. Then she said, "Marilla, do you think I'll find a best friend[1] here? I've always wanted to have a friend."

Marilla said, "Our friends, the Barrys[2] have a daughter, Diana. She is eleven like[3] you."

"Diana! What a beautiful name!" said Anne. "Her hair isn't red, is it? I hope it isn't. I hate[4] my hair. Red is so ugly[5]."

"Diana has dark hair," said Marilla.

When Anne met Diana, the two girls knew that they would be best friends.

1. **best friend** 最好的朋友
2. **the Barrys** 貝瑞家
3. **like** [laɪk] (prep.) 像；如
4. **hate** [heɪt] (v.) 討厭；嫌惡
5. **ugly** [`ʌgli] (a.) 醜的
6. **happily** [`hæpɪli] (adv.) 快樂地
7. **while** [waɪl] (conj.) 當⋯⋯
8. **soon** [suːn] (adv.) 不久地

In the morning, Anne helped Marilla around the house. Then in the afternoon, she played with Diana, or talked happily[6] with Matthew while[7] he worked on the farm.

She soon[8] knew the names of every flower, tree, and animal at Green Gables and she loved them all.

One Point Lesson

◆ **What a** beautiful name! 好美的名字啊！

What + a + 形容詞 **+** 名詞：驚嘆句。

e.g **What a** big dog (this is)!（這是隻）好大的狗呀！

One person who wanted to know everything in Avonlea was Mrs. Rachel Lynde. She was very interested in the Cuthbert's orphan[1] girl. Mrs. Lynde decided to visit Green Gables.

Marilla welcomed[2] Mrs. Lynde into the farmhouse[3], and told her all about Anne.

"So you and Matthew have decided to adopt her!" said Mrs. Lynde.

Marilla said with a smile[4], "She's a clever little thing. She's brought[5] some joy[6] and laughter[7] to this house."

But Mrs. Lynde shook her head sadly. "You've made a mistake[8], Marilla!"

1. **orphan** [ˋɔːrfən] (n.) 孤兒
2. **welcome** [ˋwelkəm] (v.) 歡迎
3. **farmhouse** [ˋfɑːrmhaʊs] (n.) 農舍
4. **with a smile** 帶著微笑
5. **bring** [brɪŋ] (v.) 帶來 (bring-brought-brought)
6. **joy** [dʒɔɪ] (n.) 歡樂
7. **laughter** [ˋlæftər] (n.) 歡笑
8. **make a mistake** 犯錯
9. **just then** 恰好那時
10. **freckle** [ˋfrekəl] (n.) 雀斑
11. **carrot** [ˋkarət] (n.) 胡蘿蔔
12. **angrily** [ˋæŋgrɪli] (adv.) 憤怒地
13. **fat** [fæt] (a.) 肥胖的
14. **terrible** [ˋterəbəl] (a.) 恐怖的
15. **upstairs** [ʌpˋsterz] (adv.) 往樓上

Just then[9], Anne ran in from the garden.
Mrs. Lynde looked at the thin, little girl.

"Isn't she thin, Marilla?" asked Mrs. Lynde.
And just look at those freckles[10], and that hair—
red as carrots[11]!"

Anne's face became very red. "I hate you!"
she shouted angrily[12]. "I hate you! You're a fat[13],
old, terrible[14] woman!" Then Anne ran upstairs[15]
to her room.

9

"Oh, dear[1], what a terrible child!" said Mrs. Lynde. You'll have a lot of problems with[2] that one. I can tell[3] you that!"

Marilla replied, "You were rude[4] to her, Rachel." Mrs. Lynde was very surprised.

"Well!" she said. "I think this orphan girl is more important to you than I am. Well, I'm sorry for you, that's all. Goodbye."

Then, Marilla went up to Anne's room. The child was lying on[5] her narrow bed. Her face was on her pillow[6], and she was crying.

"You shouldn't get angry[7] like that," Marilla said softly.

Anne lifted[8] her head and said, "She was mean[9] to me!"

1. **oh, dear** 噢，親愛的
2. **have a problem with** ……有麻煩
3. **can tell** 能辨認；能判定
4. **rude** [ruːd] (a.) 無禮的
5. **lie on** 躺在……上面 (lay-lain-lying)
6. **pillow** [ˋpɪloʊ] (n.) 枕頭
7. **get angry** 生氣；發怒
8. **lift** [lɪft] (v.) 抬起
9. **mean** [miːn] (a.) 心地不好的
10. **apologize for** 為……道歉
11. **rudeness** [ˋruːdnɪs] (n.) 無禮貌；粗魯
12. **drop down** 低下
13. **be ready to** 準備好……

"I understand how you feel," said Marilla.
"But you must go to her, and apologize for[10] your
rudeness[11]."

Anne's head dropped down[12]. "I can never do
that," she said.

"Then you must stay in your room, and think
about it," Marilla said firmly. "You can come out
when you're ready to[13] apologize."

One Point Lesson

♦ You **shouldn't** get angry like that. 你不該那樣發脾氣的。

should / must : 應該。should 和 must 為助動詞，後面應接
原形動詞。

e.g. You **should** see a doctor. 你應該看醫生。
You **must** come home by nine o'clock.
你應該在 9 點以前回到家。

Breakfast, lunch, and dinner seemed[1] very quiet without[2] Anne.

That evening, Matthew quietly went upstairs. The little girl was sitting sadly by the window.

"Anne," said Matthew, "Why don't you say you're sorry?"

"I am sorry now," said Anne. "I was very angry yesterday! But when I woke up this morning, I wasn't angry anymore. I was even[3] a little ashamed[4]. But do you really want me to . . . apologize?"

"Yes, that's the very[5] word[6]," said Matthew.

---

1. **seem** [siːm] (v.) 似乎
2. **without** [wɪˋðaʊt] (prep.) 沒有
3. **even** [ˋiːvən] (adv.) 甚至；連
4. **ashamed** [əˋʃeɪmd] (adj.)
   難為情的；羞愧的
5. **very** [ˋveri] (a.) 正是；恰好是
6. **word** [wɜːrd] (n.) 話；言詞
7. **kind** [kaɪnd] (a.) 仁慈的
8. **would** [wʊd] (aux.) 將
9. **anything** [ˋeniθɪŋ] (pron.)
   無論任何事情
10. **sigh** [saɪ] (v.) 嘆息

"I really don't want to apologize to that woman," she said. Then she looked at Matthew's kind[7] face. "But I would[8] do anything[9] for you."

Anne sighed[10]. "Ok, I'll do it."

Matthew smiled. "That's a good girl." he said.

One Point Lesson

🔹 **Why don't you** say you're sorry? 你為什麼不道歉？

Why don't you . . .? : 你為什麼不……？你可以……。
用來向別人提議或建議。

e.g. **Why don't you** read the book? 你為什麼不讀這本書？

Marilla was pleased to[1] hear that Anne would apologize. Later that evening, she and Anne visited Mrs. Lynde's house. Anne fell on her knees[2] in Mrs. Lynde's warm kitchen.

"Oh, Mrs. Lynde," cried the little girl. "I'm so sorry. I can't tell you how sorry I am, so you must just imagine it. But please say that you will forgive[3] me. I'll be sad all my life if you don't[4]!"

1. **be pleased to** 因……而高興
2. **fall on one's knees** 雙膝跪下來 (fall-fell-fallen)
3. **forgive** [fər`gɪv] (v.) 原諒 (forgive-forgave-forgiven)
4. **if you don't** 假如你不……

Marilla looked closely[5] at Anne. She thought Anne was not really sorry. However, Mrs. Lynde said kindly[6], "Of course, I forgive you, Anne. I said your hair is a terrible red, but don't worry. I had a friend once[7] who had red hair like yours. When she grew up[8], it became a beautiful brown. Now, you can go play in my garden."

When Anne was gone, Mrs. Lynde turned to[9] Marilla. "She's a strange little girl. She gets angry[10] easily, but she also cools down[11] fast. That's better than a child who hides[12] her feelings[13]. She has a strange way[14] of talking, but I think I like her."

5. **closely** [`klousli] (adv.)
   親近地;仔細地
6. **kindly** [`kaɪndli] (adv.)
   仁慈地;親切地
7. **once** [wʌns] (adv.) 曾經
8. **grow up** 長大
9. **turn to** 轉向

10. **get angry** 生氣;發怒
11. **cool down** (從怒氣中)
    冷靜下來
12. **hide** [haɪd] (v.) 隱藏
    (hide-hid-hidden)
13. **feeling** [`fiːlɪŋ] (n.) 感覺
14. **way** [weɪ] (n.) 方式;方法

A Fill in the blanks with the given words.

> pleased   ashamed   upset

❶ I was _____ when the baby suddenly began to cry.

❷ I was _____ because I told a lie to my mother.

❸ I was _____ that I passed the test.

B Choose the correct answer.

❶ Why did Anne get angry at Mrs. Lynde?

   (a) Because Mrs. Lynde said boys were better than girls.

   (b) Because Mrs. Lynde said Anne had ugly red hair.

   (c) Because Mrs. Lynde said Anne was very rude and terrible.

❷ Who convinced Anne to apologize to Mrs. Lynde?

   (a) Marilla

   (b) Diana

   (c) Matthew

C True or False.

T F **1** Anne and Diana played in the field all day long.

T F **2** Mrs. Lynde was very interested in everything in Avonlea.

T F **3** Mrs. Lynde didn't forgive Anne because Anne was not really sorry.

D Complete the sentences with "what".

This is a very beautiful name.

⇨ *What a beautiful name* **this is!**

1 This is a very tall tree.

⇨ _____ this is!

2 That is a very pretty doll.

⇨ _____ this is!!

3 She is a very nice girl.

⇨ _____ she is!

Chapter Three

🎧 12 I Hate You, Gilbert.

When school started in September, Anne and Diana walked to school together. Diana said to Anne, "Today you'll meet Gilbert Blythe. He's very good-looking[1]."

"Oh, boys!" said Anne. "I'm not interested in[2] them."

But when Anne saw Gilbert in school, she did look at him closely[3]. He was tall with curly[4] brown hair. He had a friendly[5] smile.

"He is good-looking," whispered[6] Anne to Diana.

1. **good-looking** 長相好看的
2. **be interested in**
   對……有興趣
3. **look closely** 仔細地看
4. **curly** [ˋkɜːrli] (a.)
   蜷曲的；鬈的
5. **friendly** [ˋfrendli] (a.)
   友善的；親切的
6. **whisper** [ˋwɪspər] (v.) 低語

The next day was quiet at the Avonlea school. The teacher, Mr. Philips, was in the back of[7] the classroom. He was helping some of the older children. Anne was looking out[8] the window. She was dreaming[9].

Gilbert saw her and wanted to talk to her. He whispered, "Hey, Anne!"

Anne did not hear Gilbert. She was imagining that she was flying[10] in the wind above the beautiful trees.

Gilbert was surprised. Usually girls wanted to talk to him.

7. **in the back of** 在……的後面
8. **look out** 看出去
9. **dream** [dri:m] (v.) 想像；幻想

10. **fly** [flaɪ] (v.) 飛
    (fly-flew-flown)

He reached over[1], and pulled[2] Anne's hair. "Carrots, carrots!" he yelled[3].

Anne jumped up[4], and looked at Gilbert. "What a horrible[5] boy you are!" she shouted. "I hate you!" Then she raised up[6] her book and hit Gilbert's head!

Mr. Phillips saw Anne hit Gilbert with her book. "Anne," said Mr. Phillips, "Why did you do that?"

Gilbert spoke up[7]. "It was my fault[8], Mr. Phillips. I was rude to[9] her. That's why[10] she hit me."

1. **reach over** 伸過手去
2. **pull** [pʊl] (v.) 拉
3. **yell** [jɛl] (v.) 叫喊
4. **jump up** 跳起來
5. **horrible** [ˋhɔːrəbəl] (a.) 可怕的；令人討厭的
6. **raise up** 舉起
7. **speak up** 大聲地說 (speak-spoke-spoken)
8. **fault** [fɔːlt] (n.) 錯誤
9. **be rude to** 對……無禮
10. **That's why . . .** 那就是為什麼……

Mr. Phillips was not happy with[11] Anne. "That's no excuse[12] to hit another student," he said. "Anne, go up and stand in front of[13] the class[14]."

Anne stood up in front of the class for the entire[15] afternoon. She looked[16] very angry.

"I hate Mr. Phillips," she thought. "And I hate Gilbert Blythe. I'll never look at, or speak to him again!"

11. **be happy with . . .**
　　對⋯⋯感到高興
12. **no excuse** 不可原諒
13. **in front of** 在⋯⋯的前面
14. **class** [klæs] (n.) 教室；班級

15. **entire** [ɪn`taɪr] (a.) 全部的
16. **look** + 形容詞
　　看起來⋯⋯

One Point Lesson

◆ That's **no excuse to hit** another student.
　打另一個學生是不可原諒的。

___

to 可放在不同的名詞後面，表達各種不同的關係。

e.g. I have **nothing to say.** 我無話可說。

The next day, some of the boy students were playing in a field[1] during lunch. They were late for afternoon class. Anne ran into[2] the class with them, right behind[3] Mr. Phillips.

"You're late," said Mr. Phillips. "You won't[4] sit with Diana today. I see that[5] you enjoy being with the boys. So you'll sit next to Gilbert this afternoon."

"He can't be[6] serious[7]!" she thought. But Mr. Phillips was serious. "Did you hear me, Anne?" he said.

"Yes, sir," Anne said softly[8].

1. **field** [fiːld] (n.) 運動場
2. **run into** 跑進……
3. **right behind** 就在……背後
4. **won't =will not** 將不
5. **I see that . . .** 我了解……
6. **can't be** 一定不是
7. **serious** 認真的；當真的
8. **softly** [ˋsɒːftli] (adv.) 輕柔地
9. **pick up** 撿起
10. **seem to** + 原形動詞 似乎；感覺好像
11. **last** [læst] (v.) 持續；維持
12. **forever** [fərˋevər] (adv.) 永遠

She picked up⁹ her books and moved slowly to the desk next to Gilbert. Then she sat down and put her head on the desk.

"I wasn't the only person who was late." thought Anne.

"Why did Mr. Phillips make me sit with a boy? And the worst boy is Gilbert Blythe!"

That afternoon seemed to¹⁰ last¹¹ forever¹² for Anne.

One Point Lesson

♦ Why did Mr. Philips **make me sit** with a boy?
為什麼菲利浦先生要叫我和一個男孩坐在一起？

make + 受詞 + 原形動詞：使……做……

e.g. He **made us clean** the classroom. 他叫我們打掃教室。

When school was over[1], Anne went back to her desk. She picked up all her books, pens and pencils.

"What are you doing?" asked Diana.

"I'm not coming back to[2] school," said Anne.

"Oh, no! But Anne, we're going to[3] read a new book! And we'll play a game[4] on Monday. It'll be very exciting[5]!" But Anne didn't care[6].

That evening, Marilla visited Mrs. Lynde.

"Rachel, please give me some advice! Anne says she's not going back to school! What should I say to her?"

Of course, Mrs. Lynde already knew all about Anne's troubles[7] at school.

1. **be over** 結束
2. **come back to** 回來……
3. **be going to** 將要……
4. **play a game** 玩遊戲
5. **exciting** [ɪk`saɪtɪŋ] (a.) 令人興奮的；刺激的
6. **care** [ker] (v.) 在乎
7. **trouble** [`trʌbəl] (n.) 麻煩
8. **raise** [reɪz] (v.) 養育；撫養
9. **don't worry** 別擔心
10. **leave A alone** 別打擾 A

"Well, Marilla," said Mrs. Lynde, "I've raised[8] ten children myself. So I can tell you don't worry[9]. Leave Anne alone[10]. She'll want to go back to school soon."

So Marilla did nothing, and Anne stayed at home.

One Point Lesson

◆ We**'re going to** read a new book. 我們將要讀一本新書。

be going to + 原形動詞：將要……
表示未來會發生或計畫做的事。

e.g. I**'m going to** travel around the world.
　　我將要去環遊世界。

One day, Marilla found Anne crying in the kitchen. "What's the matter[1], child?" asked Marilla in surpise[2].

"I miss[3] Diana very much," sobbed[4] Anne. "I can't live without her, Marilla! But what will happen when she gets married[5]? I hate her husband already! I can imagine her in church with her white dress. She'll leave me then! And I'll never see her again!"

Anne of Green Gables

Marilla tried not to laugh, but she couldn't help[6] it. She laughed and laughed. Anne raised her head and stared at[7] Marilla. Suddenly, she felt very foolish[8].

The next day, Anne went back to school. All the children were very happy to see her again, especially[9] Diana. However, Anne did not speak to Gilbert Blythe. She was still mad at[10] him, and she thought she would never forgive[11] him.

1. **matter** [`mætər] (n.)
   事情；問題
2. **in surprise** 驚訝
3. **miss** [mɪs] (v.) 想念；惦記
4. **sob** [sɑ:b] (v.) 啜泣
5. **get married** 結婚
6. **cannot help** 克制不住

7. **stare at** 盯著；凝視
8. **foolish** [`fu:lɪʃ] 愚蠢的
9. **especially** [ɪ`speʃəli] (adv.)
   尤其地
10. **be mad at** 對……很惱怒
11. **forgive** [fər`gɪv] (v.) 寬恕

One Point Lesson

◊ I can't live **without** her. 我不能沒有她。

---

without 後面接：名詞或動詞（V-ing）

e.g. I can do it **without** your help.
沒有你的幫助，我無法完成。
He went out **without saying** a word.
他連句話都沒說就出門了。

A Fill in the blanks with prepositions.

❶ The teacher was _____ the back of the classroom.
Anne stood up _____ front of the class.

❷ Anne jumped _____ and shouted.
Anne picked _____ her books and moved slowly.

❸ Anne raised her head and stared _____ Marilla.
Anne was still mad _____ Gilbert.

B Fill in the blanks with the given words.

horrible   serious   friendly   exciting

❶ Gilbert was good-looking and had a _____ smile.

❷ What a _____ boy you are! I hate you!

❸ We'll play a game on Monday. It'll be _____!

❹ Mr. Phillips wasn't joking. He was _____.

C Fill in the blanks according to the story.

❶ How did Gilbert make Anne angry?

⇨ He _____ Anne's hair and called her _____.

❷ How did Mr. Phillips punish Anne for being late?

⇨ He made Anne _____ _____ _____ Gilbert.

❸ Why did Marilla visit Mrs. Lynde?

⇨ To get Mrs. Lynde's _____ about Anne's troubles.

D True or False.

T F ❶ When Anne saw Gilbert in school, she hated him at first sight.

T F ❷ Mrs. Lynde told Marilla to leave Anne alone and not to worry.

T F ❸ Anne thought she couldn't live without Diana.

Before You Read

roof
屋頂

bright green leaves
發亮的綠色樹葉

farm
農場

branch
樹枝

almost sixty years old
將近60歲

old and shy
年老且靦腆

warm smile
溫暖的微笑

Matthew
馬修

terrace
露臺

grass
草地

red curly hair
紅色鬈髮

freckles
雀斑

Anne
安妮

small and
white face
小巧白淨的臉蛋

beautiful hat
with lots of flowers
有許多花朵的美麗帽子

thin
瘦的

help around the house
幫忙整理房子

beautiful dress
美麗的洋裝

do the house work
做家事

imagine
想像

shoes
鞋子

imagination
想像力

get angry easily and cool down fast
容易動怒，也很快冷靜下來

Chapter Four

🎧17 Anne's Mistakes

One day, Marilla announced[1], "I'll ask[2] the new vicar[3], Mr. Allan and his wife to my tea party[4] on Wednesday." Anne was very excited.

"Mrs. Allan is beautiful, and she has a sweet smile! I'd like to[5] make a cake for her. Can I, please?"

"All right, you can make a cake for her," said Marilla.

Wednesday finally came, and everyone was sitting around having tea. Marilla had made many small cakes to go with[6] Anne's special cake.

1. **announce** [ə`naʊns] (v.) 宣佈
2. **ask** A **to** B 邀請A到B來
3. **vicar** [`vɪkər] (n.) 教區牧師
4. **tea party** 茶會
5. **I'd like to** 我想要
6. **go with** 與……相配

"These are very good cakes, Mrs. Cuthbert," said Mrs. Allan.

"It[7] was my pleasure[8]," said Marilla. "But I didn't make all of them. Here, try[9] this one. Anne made it especially for you."

Mrs. Allan took the cake and ate some. Suddenly[10], there was a strange look[11] on her face.

"Is anything wrong?" asked Marilla. Quickly she ate a piece of[12] Anne's cake.

"Oh no, Anne! What did you put[13] in this cake?" Anne's face turned red[14].

7. **It was my pleasure.**
   這是我的榮幸。
8. **pleasure** [ˋplɛʒər] (n.)
   愉快;高興
9. **try** [traɪ] (v.) 嘗試
10. **suddenly** [ˋsʌdnlɪ] (adv.)
    突然地
11. **look** [lʊk] (n.) 表情;臉色
12. **a piece of** 一塊……
13. **put** [pʊt] (v.) 放
    (put-put-put)
14. **turn red** 變紅

"What's the matter . . . don't you like it?" asked Anne.

"Like it? It's horrible[1]!" Marilla said. "Don't eat anymore[2], Mrs. Allan! Anne, you put my medicine[3] in this cake!"

"Oh, I didn't know!" said Anne. It was white, and in a bottle! I thought it was milk!"

Anne felt tears[4] in her eyes, and she ran upstairs to her bed.

1. **horrible** [`hɔ:rəbəl] (a.)
   可怕的

2. **anymore** [`enimɔ:r] (adv.)
   再也（不）

3. **medicine** [`medɪsən] (n.) 藥

4. **tear** [tɪr] (n.) 眼淚

She did not come down to say goodbye to the Allans.

After everyone left, Marilla came up to Anne's room.

"Oh, Marilla," cried Anne. "I'm so embarrassed[5]!"

Marilla smiled, and wiped[6] the tears from Anne's face.

"Mrs. Allan wasn't angry," said Marilla. "She said it was very kind of you to[7] make her a cake!"

Anne stopped crying. "Oh, she's forgiven me, hasn't she? She's so nice!"

Then Anne frowned[8]. "Why do I always make mistakes[9] like this?"

"Oh, you'll make plenty more[10] mistakes," said Marilla with a smile. "You're very good at[11] making mistakes!"

5. **embarrassed** [ɪmˋbærəst] (a.)
   尷尬的；困窘的
6. **wipe** [waɪp] (v.) 擦拭
7. **be kind of** *A* **to**
   A 對……很親切

8. **frown** [fraʊn] (v.)
   皺眉；表示不滿
9. **make a mistake** 犯錯
10. **plenty more** 更多
11. **be good at** 擅長

19

One April evening, Marilla came home late after visiting friends. She went upstairs to see Anne.

"Don't look at me, Marilla!" Anne cried. "I know I'm bad. I know I am!"

"What's the matter?" asked Marilla.

"Oh, Marilla, I just want to die[1]!" sobbed[2] Anne. "Look at my hair!"

Then Marilla noticed[3] that Anne's red hair was now a horrible dark green[4]!

"Oh, Anne!" yelled Marilla. "What have you done now?"

Anne explained as she tried not to cry. "I bought a bottle[5] of something from a man who came to the door. He said it would change my hair from red to[6] black! Oh, it was stupid[7] of me to believe[8] him!"

1. **die** [daɪ] (v.) 死亡
2. **sob** [sɑːb] (v.) 啜泣
3. **notice** [ˋnoutɪs] (v.) 注意
4. **dark green** [dɑːrk griːn] 深綠色
5. **bottle** [ˋbɑːtl] (n.) 瓶
6. **change** *A* **from . . . to . . .** 把 A 從……改變成為……
7. **stupid** [ˋstjuːpɪd] (a.) 愚蠢的
8. **believe** [bɪˋliːv] (v.) 相信

It was stupid of me to believe him!
我真愚蠢，竟然會相信他。

It is + (adj.) + of + A +　to：A……，真……

It 可以當做虛主詞，放在句首代表之後要提到的狀況。

e.g. It is careless of her to make the mistake.
她真粗心，竟然犯這個錯。

20

Marilla washed Anne's hair again and again[1], but it was still[2] green. Anne stayed at home for a whole[3] week. She didn't see anybody except[4] Marilla and Matthew.

At the end of the week, Marilla finally said, "I'm sorry, Anne, but you can't stay home forever. And you can't go to school with green hair. We'll have to cut it all off [5]."

"I guess[6] you're right," said Anne sadly. "Maybe[7] this will teach me not to think about being beautiful."

1. **again and again** 再三地
2. **still** [stɪl] (adv.) 仍然；還是
3. **whole** [houl] (a.) 全部的
4. **except** [ɪk`sept] (prep.) 除了……之外
5. **cut off** 剪掉 (cut-cut-cut)
6. **guess** [ges] (v.) 猜
7. **maybe** [`meɪbi] (adv.) 或許
8. **in** [ɪn] (prep.) 在……以後

Chapter Four
Anne's Mistakes

The next day at school, everyone was surprised to see Anne's hair so short. They asked what happened, but Anne didn't say anything.

In[8] just a few weeks, Anne started growing some new, darker red curls. This made Anne happy.

◆ Maybe this will teach me **not to think** about being beautiful.
或許這教會了我，不要妄想會變美麗。

形成否定的不定詞時，把 not 放在 to 的前面。

e.g. I tried **not to cry**. 我試著不哭出來。

21

That summer, Anne and her friends played by the river. They found an old boat there. Anne had an idea.

"Let's imagine that I am a prisoner[1], and I'm escaping from[2] prison[3] by boat." Anne told her friends. "I'll hide in the boat, and the river will carry it down[4] to the bridge[5]. You pretend[6] to be my family, and wait by the bridge."

The other girls agreed, so Anne got on[7] the boat. Then they pushed[8] the boat into the river.

Anne was very excited about being a prisoner. Suddenly, however, she felt wet. There was water in the bottom[9] of the boat! Water was coming into the boat, and it was sinking[10]!

1. **prisoner** [ˈprɪzənər] (n.) 囚犯
2. **escape from** 從……脫逃
3. **prison** [ˈprɪzən] (n.) 牢獄
4. **carry down** 運送下來
5. **bridge** [brɪdʒ] (n.) 橋
6. **pretend** [prɪˈtend] (v.) 假裝
7. **get on** 登上（車或船）
8. **push** [pʊʃ] (v.) 推；推進
9. **bottom** [ˈbɑːtəm] (n.) 底部
10. **sink** [sɪŋk] (v.) 下沉 (sink-sank-sunk)
11. **look around** 四下張望
12. **afraid** [əˈfreɪd] (a.) 害怕的
13. **drown** [draʊn] (v.) 溺水
14. **scream** [skriːm] (v.) 尖叫

Anne looked around[11] quickly. She saw some trees by the river. She jumped up and caught a branch.

Anne's friends were waiting on the bridge. They saw the boat come around the corner and sink.

They were afraid[12] because they did not see Anne. "Anne's drowned[13]!" they screamed[14]. The girls ran to the village to get help.

22

Poor Anne was in trouble[1]. She was hanging[2] by her arms from a branch over the river.

"I've got you!" Suddenly, she heard a familiar voice. Anne saw Gilbert Blythe in his boat. Quickly, he helped Anne into the boat.

When they arrived at the bridge, Anne got out of[3] the boat and turned away[4].
"Thank you." she said coldly[5].
"Anne," he said quickly. "I'm sorry I called you 'carrots.' It was a long time ago. I think your hair is really nice now. Can we forget it, and be friends?"

For a second[6], Anne wanted to say yes. Suddenly she remembered standing in front of the class because of Gilbert.

1. **be in trouble** 惹上麻煩
2. **hang** [hæŋ] (v.) 懸掛 (hang-hung-hung)
3. **get out of** 從……出來
4. **turn away** 轉過去
5. **coldly** [ˋkoʊldli] (adv.) 冷淡地
6. **for a second** 一瞬間
7. **proudly** [ˋpraʊdli] (adv.) 驕傲地；得意地
8. **strangely** [ˋstreɪndʒli] (adv.) 奇怪地；怪異地

"No," she replied coldly. "I can never be your friend, Gilbert Blythe!"

Gilbert got angry. "All right, then!" he said. "I'll never ask you again, Anne Shirley!"

Anne walked home proudly[7], but she felt strangely[8] sad, and wanted to cry.

◆ Suddenly she **remembered standing** in front of the class because of Gilbert.
突然她想起來曾因吉爾伯特，害她被罰站在教室前面。

---

remember + V-ing：記得曾……（已經做過的事）
remember + to + (v.)：記得要去……（尚未做的事）

e.g. I **remembered meeting** her on Sunday.
我記得星期天和她見面的事。
I **remembered to meet** her on Sunday.
我記得星期天要去見她。

A Fill in the blanks according to the story.

❶ Mr. Allan was the new _____ of Avonlea.

❷ Anne felt _____ in her eyes.

❸ Anne pretended to be an escaped _____.

❹ They thought Anne had _____
because they didn't see Anne in the boat.

1 sevicariou

2 autrtearsou

3 biprisonerounder

4 uncldrownediearoy

B Rearrange the sentences in chronological order.

❶ Anne jumped up and caught a branch.

❷ Anne's friends saw the boat sink.

❸ Gilbert helped Anne into the boat.

❹ Anne's friends hid Anne in the boat.

❺ Water came into the boat.

_____ ⇨ _____ ⇨ _____ ⇨ _____ ⇨ _____

C Choose the correct answer.

1 What mistake did Anne make when she made a cake?

(a) She used sour milk.

(b) She put Marilla's medicine in the cake.

(c) She forgot to put milk in the cake.

2 Why did Anne hide in the boat?

(a) She and her friends were playing a game.

(b) She didn't want Gilbert to see her.

(c) She was escaping from school.

D Choose the correct answer about Anne.

(a) Anne was very careful and thought a lot before doing something.

(b) Anne didn't care about what other people thought of her.

(c) Anne made a lot of mistakes just like any other young person.

Chapter Five

🎧 23 # You Did It!

One day, Marilla told Anne that Miss Stacey, a new teacher, had come to Green Gables.

"Anne, she thinks you are doing well[1] in school. If you study well, you can pass[2] the examination[3] for Queen's College in Charlottetown. Then, after a year at the college, you can become a teacher!"

Anne was very happy. "Oh, I'd love to be a teacher!"

So in the afternoons, Anne and some of her friends stayed late at school. Miss Stacey helped them prepare for the exam.

1. **do well** 表現良好
2. **pass** [pæs] (v.) 通過
3. **examination** [ɪgˌzæmɪˈneɪʃən] (n.) 考試 (= exam)
4. **each other** 互相；彼此
5. **enemy** [ˈenəmi] (n.) 敵人
6. **score** [skɔːr] (n.) 分數

Diana didn't want to go to Queen's college, so she went home early. However, Gilbert stayed at school with Anne. He and Anne did not speak to each other[4].

Everyone knew that they were enemies[5]. Both of them wanted to get the highest score[6] on the exam. Secretly Anne wished that she and Gilbert were friends, but it was too late now.

One Point Lesson

◆ Miss Stacey **helped them prepare** for the exam.
史黛希小姐幫助他們準備考試。

help + 受詞 + 原形動詞：幫忙……做……

e.g. My brother **helped me do** my homework.
我哥哥幫助我做回家作業。

One day, Mrs. Lynde visited Marilla. "Your Anne is a big girl[1] now," said Mrs. Lynde. "She's taller than you!"

"You're right, Rachel," said Marilla.

"Well, she certainly[2] has grown into[3] a nice young woman," said Mrs. Lynde. "Those beautiful gray[4] eyes, and that red-brown hair! You've looked after[5] her very well."

"Well, thank you," said Marilla. Marilla was very pleased[6] and proud[7].

Later, that evening, Matthew found Marilla crying quietly in the kitchen.

"Marilla, what happened?" asked Matthew.

"Nothing happened," said Marilla. "I'm just thinking that I will miss Anne when she goes away[8]."

Matthew was surprised. "You mean when she goes to college? Don't be sad, Marilla. She'll be back[9] on the weekends and for holidays."

"I'll still[10] miss her," said Marilla sadly.

1. **a big girl** 大女孩;長大的女孩
2. **certainly** [`sɜ:rtnli] (adv.) 確實
3. **grow into** 長大成為
   (grow-grew-grown)
4. **gray** [greɪ] (a.) 灰色的
5. **look after** 照顧

6. **pleased** [pli:zd] (a.) 高興的
7. **proud** [praʊd] (a.) 驕傲的
8. **go away** 離開
9. **be back** 回來
10. **still** [stɪl] (adv.) 仍然;還是

🎧 25

The time passed[1] quickly. On a warm summer day in early June, Anne took the exam.

That afternoon, Anne returned to[2] Green Gables. She was still nervous[3].
"Oh, I hope I did well," she said. "The exams were very difficult! And I have to wait for three weeks before I know!"

Diana was the first to hear the news. She ran into the kitchen at Green Gables, waving[4] a newspaper. "Look Anne!" she shouted. "You came in first[5]! And Gilbert passed[6], too!"

Anne took the paper with shaking[7] hands. She saw her name on top of[8] a list[9] of two hundred students.

1. **pass** [pas] (v.) 流逝；推移
2. **return to** [rɪ`tɜːrn tu] 回到
3. **nervous** [`nɜːrvəs] (a.) 緊張的
4. **wave** [weɪv] (v.) 揮
5. **come in first**
   第一個出現；得到第一名
6. **pass** [pas] (v.) 通過
7. **shake** [ʃeɪk] (v.) 顫抖
   (shake-shook-shaken)
8. **on top of** 在……的首位
9. **list** [lɪst] (n.) 列表
10. **for the first time** 第一次

For the first time[10] in her life, she could not speak. "Well, now, I knew you would do it," said Matthew with a warm smile.

"You've done well, Anne," said Marilla. They were very pleased.

One Point Lesson

♦ "Well, now, I knew you would do it," said Matthew **with a warm smile**. 馬修帶著溫暖的微笑說:「好,妳看,我就知道妳會做到的。」

---

with a warm smile:帶著溫暖的微笑
with + 名詞:帶著……。用來修飾前面的名詞。

e.g. "I am so sorry," he said **with a sigh**.
他嘆息著說:「我很抱歉。」

26

For the next three weeks, Anne and Marilla were very busy. Anne needed new dresses to wear to college.

The evening before she left, Anne put on[1] one of the dresses to show[2] Matthew. Marilla watched, too. She remembered the thin, little girl who showed up[3] by mistake[4] five years ago. Marilla started to cry.

"Why are you crying?" asked Anne.
"I was just thinking of[5] you when you were a little girl," said Marilla.
"And, now you're going away[6]. . . , and I'll . . . I'll be lonely[7] without you."

Anne took Marilla's hands. "Marilla, nothing will change," she said. "I may be bigger and older now, but I'll always be your little Anne. And I will love you and Matthew and Green Gables more and more[8] every day."

1. **put on** 穿上 (put-put-put)
2. **show** [ʃou] (v.) 展現；展示
3. **show up** 出現
4. **by mistake** 錯誤地
5. **think of** 想到
6. **go away** 離開
7. **lonely** [ˋlounli] (a.) 孤獨的
8. **more and more** 愈來愈

One Point Lesson

◆ The evening before she left, Anne **put on** one of the dresses
to show Matthew.
安妮離家的前一晚，她穿上洋裝給馬修看。

put on 和 wear 的差異：
put on 是「穿上」、「戴上」的意思，可用於穿衣服、穿鞋、戴帽
等，著重於穿的動作。
wear 是「穿著、戴著」，強調穿著的狀態。

e.g. He **put on** a coat to go out. 他穿上外套就出去了。
She was **wearing** a blouse and a skirt.
她穿著襯衫和裙子。

27

For the next year, Anne lived in Charlottetown, and went to college every day. Gilbert was also at Queen's, and sometimes Anne saw him. However, she didn't want to be the first to speak to him. Gilbert never looked at her.

At the end of the year, there were exams. "I'd love to get[1] the highest score," she thought. "Or perhaps[2] I could get the Avery prize[3]."

The Avery prize was given to the student who wrote the best essay[4]. She wanted the Avery prize, because the student who won[5] the Avery prize also won a four-year scholarship[6] to Redmond College. This university was one of the best in Canada.

1. **get** [gɛt] (v.) 獲得；贏得
2. **perhaps** [pəˋhæps] (adv.) 也許；可能
3. **prize** [praɪz] (n.) 獎項
4. **essay** [ˋɛseɪ] (n.) 短文；散文
5. **win** [wɪn] (v.) 贏得 (win-won-won)
6. **scholarship** [ˋskɑːlərʃɪp] (n.) 獎學金

On the day the results[7] of the exams were announced[8], Anne was afraid to check[9] herself. Instead, she heard her friends shouting. "It's Gilbert," they shouted. "He got the highest score on the exam!" Anne felt sick[10].

Then she heard her own name. "Anne won the Avery prize!" Then all her friends were around her, laughing and shouting. "Matthew and Marilla will be happy," thought Anne.

7. **result** [rɪˋzʌlt] (n.) 結果
8. **announce** [əˋnaʊns] (v.) 宣佈
9. **check** [tʃek] (v.) 檢查;核對
10. **feel sick** 覺得不愉快

A Fill in the blanks with the given words.

> because   however   before

❶ Diana went home early. _____ Gilbert stayed at school with Anne.

❷ I have to wait for three weeks _____ I know the result.

❸ Anne wanted to get the highest score _____ she wanted to please them.

B Match.

❶ Anne _____ well in school.   •   • ⓐ came

❷ Miss Stacy thought Anne _____ a   •   • ⓑ took
chance to go to Queen's college.

❸ Anne _____ the examination.   •   • ⓒ did

❹ Anne saw her name on top of a list of •   • ⓓ had
two hundred students. She _____ in
first.

C Choose the correct answer.

1 Anne studied hard because she wanted to be
_____.

(a) a doctor

(b) a teacher

(c) a famous writer

2 Marilla felt sad about Anne's going to college
because _____.

(a) Anne would not be a big help around the house

(b) she thought she would miss Anne

(c) Anne would not come back to Green Gables

D True or False.

T F **1** Anne and Gilbert got the same score on the
Queen's college entrance exam.

T F **2** Anne and Gilbert had interesting conversations
at college.

T F **3** If Anne won the Avery prize, she wouldn't need
money for school.

Chapter Six

🎧28 Matthew and Marilla

But when Anne arrived back at Green Gables, she felt something was wrong. Matthew looked much older than before.

"What's the matter with him?" Anne asked Marilla.

"He's had some heart problems this year," replied Marilla.

"And you don't look well[1], yourself" said Anne.

"My head. It hurts[2] often, behind[3] my eyes." Marilla paused[4]. "But, there's another thing, Anne. Have you heard anything about the Church Bank?"

"I heard it was having some problems," replied Anne.

"Yes," said Marilla. "Well, all of our money is in that bank. I know Matthew is worried about[5] it."

---

1. **well** [wel] (a.) 好的；健康的
2. **hurt** [hɜːrt] (v.) 傷害
   (hurt-hurt-hurt)
3. **behind** [bɪˋhaɪnd] (prep.)
   在……後面
4. **pause** [pɒːz] (v.) 暫停；中斷

The next day, a letter came for Matthew.
He opened it and his face turned[6] gray[7].

"What's the matter?" cried Marilla. Anne also
saw Matthew's face.

Suddenly, Matthew dropped[8] to the ground.
Anne and Marilla tried to wake Matthew. But they
were too late. Matthew was dead.

5. **be worried about** 擔心
6. **turn** [tɜːrn] (v.) 轉變

7. **gray** [greɪ] (a.)
   臉因恐懼而蒼白的
8. **drop** [drɑːp] (v.) 掉下；落下

When the doctor came, he said, "It was his heart. Did he have some bad news lately[1]?"

"The letter!" cried Anne. "Let's look at it. Oh, Marilla, look! The Church Bank closed down[2]! All their customers[3] lost[4] their money! Your money, and Matthew's, is all gone!"

Everyone in Avonlea was sorry to hear that Matthew died. At first[5], Anne could not cry. But then she remembered Matthew's smiling face when she told him about the Avery prize.

Suddenly, she started crying and couldn't stop. Marilla hugged[6] her, and they sobbed[7] together.

"Crying can't bring him back[8]," whispered[9] Marilla. "We'll have to learn[10] to live without him, Anne."

1. **lately** [`leɪtli] (adv.) 近來
2. **close down** 關閉；停業
3. **customer** [`kʌstəmər] (n.) 顧客
4. **lose** [luːz] (v.) 喪失；損失 (lose-lost-lost)
5. **at first** 首先
6. **hug** [hʌg] (v.) 緊抱；擁抱
7. **sob** [saːb] (v.) 啜泣
8. **bring** A **black** 把 A 帶回來；使 A 活過來
9. **whisper** [`wɪspər] (v.) 低語；低聲說
10. **learn** [lɜːrn] (v.) 學習；學會

A few days later, Marilla said, "I'll miss[1] you when you go to Redmond College, Anne. What are the other Avonlea students going to do?"

"Some will teach, and others are going to stay at Queen's," replied Anne.

"What about[2] Gilbert?" asked Marilla. "Isn't he going to teach at Avonlea school?"

Anne did not say anything. Marilla continued, "He's tall and good-looking now, don't you think? Like his father, John. You know, John and I were very good friends, years ago."

Anne was surprised. "What happened? Why didn't you . . . ?"

"Well, we had a fight[3]," said Marilla. "I forgot about what. He asked me to[4] be friends again, but I couldn't forgive him. Later, I was sorry, but he didn't speak to me again. If we had . . . Oh, well, it was a long time ago."

---

1. **miss** [mɪs] (v.) 想念
2. **What about . . . ?**
   那……呢？
3. **have a fight** 爭吵；爭論
4. **ask** *A* **to** 邀請 A……

Some will teach, and others are going to stay at Queen's.
有些人教書，有些人會繼續化王后大學。

Some . . . others . . . ：一些……，一些……
One . . . the other ：一個……，其他……
One . . . another ：一個……，另一個……

e.g. One left, **the other** stayed. 一個人離開，其他人留下來了。

The next day, Marilla went to the doctor's[1]. When she came back, she looked tired and sick.

"What did the doctor say?" asked Anne.

"If I'm not careful[2], I will be blind[3] in six months[4]!"

Anne was shocked[5]. She couldn't say anything. "Don't worry about me," said Marilla. "I think I will have to sell[6] the farm." Marilla started crying.

That night, Anne sat alone in her bedroom. She thought and thought for a long time. Before she went to sleep[7], she had made a plan.

The next morning, Anne told her plan to Marilla.

"You can't sell Green Gables. It's our home! Just listen, I have a great idea. I won't go to Redmond College; it's too far away[8]. Instead I'm going to teach in one of the village schools near here. Then I can live there during the week, and come home on the weekends to help you. It's a good plan, isn't it?"

1. **the doctor's** 醫院；診所
2. **careful** [ˋkeəfəl] (a.) 小心的
3. **blind** [blaɪnd] (a.) 盲的
4. **in six months** 六個月之後
   （in + 一段時間：……之後）
5. **shocked** [ʃɑːkt] (a.) 震驚的
6. **sell** [sɛl] (v.) 賣
7. **go to sleep** 上床睡覺
8. **far away** 遙遠的

One Point Lesson

♦ Then I can live there during the week, and come home **on the weekends** to help you.
這樣我就可以星期一到五住在那裡，週末回家來幫您的忙。

On the weekends：在週末
weekend 在字尾加上 s，代表每個週末，不特定指哪個週末。

e.g. I go to church **on Sundays.** 我星期天都會去做禮拜。
I take a nap **in the afternoons.** 我下午都會睡個午覺。

"Oh, Anne," said Marilla. "Everything will be all right if you stay here. But you must go to Redmond if you want to study . . ."

"Redmond doesn't matter[1]," laughed Anne. "I will be a really good teacher. That's the best that I can do anyway[2]!"

Marilla shook her head[3], and tried not to cry. "You're a good girl, Anne."

A few days later[4], Mrs. Lynde came to visit. She had some good news.

"Did you know that Gilbert decided to leave his job[5]?" she said.

"Why did he do that?" asked Anne.

"When he heard about your plans, he decided to give up[6] his job," said Mrs. Lynde. "That way[7], you can be the teacher at Avonlea. Then you can live at Green Gables."

"Oh!" said Anne, surprised. "That's very nice of him!"

1. **matter** [ˈmatər] (v.)
   有關係；要緊
2. **anyway** [ˈeniweɪ] (adv.)
   無論如何
3. **shake one's head** 搖頭
   (shake-shook-shaken)
4. **later** [ˈleɪtər] (adv.) 之後
5. **leave one's job** 離職
   (leave-left-left)
6. **give up** 放棄
7. **that way** 這樣的話

Later that day, Anne was walking by the river. She saw Gilbert. Anne stopped and waved at[1] him.

"Gilbert," she said softly[2]. "What you did was very sweet. Thank you very much."

"I'm happy to help you, Anne," said Gilbert. "Are we going to be friends now? Have you forgiven me for[3] calling you 'carrots'?"

Anne laughed. "I forgave you a long time ago," she said.

"I'm sure we're going to be very good friends," said Gilbert. "Can I walk[4] you home?"

1. **wave at** 向……揮手
2. **softly** [ˋsɒːftli] (adv.) 輕聲地
3. **forgive A for B**
   原諒A 關於B 的這件事
4. **walk** [wɒːk] (v.) 走路
5. **each other** 互相
6. **keep** [kiːp] (v.) 擁有；持有

When Anne came into the kitchen at Green Gables, Marilla said, "You look very happy, Anne. Was that Gilbert who came home with you?"

"Yes, Marilla," said Anne. Her face was red. "Gilbert and I decided to be friends. Oh, Marilla, I think life is going to be good for all of us! We have each other[5], and we'll keep[6] our Green Gables! What could be better than that?"

One Point Lesson

● **What you did** was very sweet. 你所做的真是太令人窩心了。

what + 主詞 + 詞：what 是複合關係代名詞，可以代替 the thing(s) which/that 或 anything that。

e.g. **What he said** was true. 他說的是真的。
Eat **what you like.** 吃你喜歡吃的。

A Choose the correct answer.

1 When Anne heard about Marilla's troubles, she decided _____.

(a) to go to Redmond College

(b) to get a teaching job near Green Gables

(c) to work on the farm

2 Gilbert helped Anne by _____.

(a) giving her some money

(b) buying her the farm

(c) giving up his job at Avonlea

B True or False.

T F **1** Matthew died because he was shocked to know his money was all gone.

T F **2** Marilla had to be careful so that she would not go blind.

T F **3** Anne never forgave Gilbert for calling her 'carrots'.

Appendixes

1 Basic Grammar

2 Guide to Listening Comprehension

3 Listening Guide

4 Listening Comprehension

1 Basic Grammar

要增強英文閱讀理解能力，應練習找出英文的主結構。
要擁有良好的英語閱讀能力，首先要理解英文的段落結構。

「英文的閱讀理解從「分解文章」開始」

　　英文的文章是以「有意義的詞組」（指帶有意義的語句）所構成的。下面以不同顏色方塊，來區別各個意義語塊，請試著掌握其中的意義。

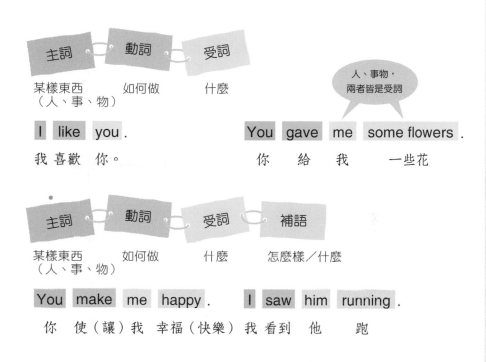

其他修飾語或副詞等，都可以視為為了完成句子而臨時、額外、特別附加的，閱讀起來便可更加輕鬆；先具備這些基本概念，再閱讀《清秀佳人》的部分精選篇章，最後做理解文章整體架構的練習。

Matthew was shocked.
馬修 是 震驚的

"A little girl? But we were expecting a boy!"
一位女孩？ 但 我們 在等待 一位男孩

Matthew and Marilla had decided to adopt
馬修和瑪瑞拉 已經決定 收養

a boy from an orphanage.
一位男孩 從孤兒院來

Matthew wanted someone to help him on the farm.
馬修 需要 人手 幫忙 他 在農場上

Matthew saw a thin girl with red hair.
馬修 看到一位纖瘦的女孩 留著紅頭髮

She saw Matthew looking at her and ran to him.
她 看到 馬修 正在看 著她 然後 跑 去他那裡

"Are you Mr. Cuthbert of Green Gables?"
是 你 卡斯伯特先生 綠色小屋的

Before Matthew could reply, she continued talking.
馬修還沒回答前 她 繼續 說

"I 'm very excited to meet you," she said.
我 是 非常 興奮的 認識你 她說

"I was really happy to hear that you wanted to adopt me."
我 是 真的 高興的 聽到你們要收養我

Matthew didn't know what to say.
馬修 不知道 要說些什麼

He felt sorry for the little girl.
他 覺得 抱歉 對這小女孩

Matthew decided to take the girl home.
馬修 決定 帶 這女孩 回家

"Marilla could tell her it was a mistake." he thought.
瑪瑞拉 一定會告訴 她 它是一個錯誤 他想

However, Matthew enjoyed listening to her
然而 馬修 享受 聽 她說的話

on the way back home.
在回家的路上

She talked a lot!
她 說話 很多

Matthew didn't have to say anything .
馬修 不必說 任何話

Marilla was pleased to hear that Anne would apologize.
瑪瑞拉 是 高興的 聽到 安妮會去道歉

Later that evening, she and Anne visited Mrs. Lynde's house .
那天晚上較晚時 她和安妮 拜訪 林德夫人的家

Anne fell on her knees in Mrs. Lynde's warm kitchen.
安妮 雙膝跪下 在林德夫人溫暖的廚房裡

"Oh, Mrs. Lynde," cried the little girl.
噢，林德夫人 這個小女孩哭著說

" I 'm so sorry . I can't tell you how sorry I am ,
我 是 多麼 難過 我 無法告訴 你 我有多難過

so you must just imagine it .
所以你 就要 想像 它

But please say that you will forgive me .
但請 說 你會原諒我

I 'll be sad all my life if you don't!"
我 將是 悲傷的 一輩子 假如你沒有原諒我

Marilla looked closely at Anne .
瑪瑞拉 看著 仔細地 安妮

She thought Anne was not really sorry
她 覺得 安妮不是真的覺得難過

Guide to Listening Comprehension

 When listening to the story, use some of the techniques shown below. If you take time to study some phonetic characteristics of English, listening will be easier.

Get in the flow of English.

English creates a rhythm formed by combinations of strong and weak stress intonations. Each word has its particular stress that combines with other words to form the overall pattern of stress or rhythm in a particular sentence.

When you are speaking and listening to English, it is essential to get in the flow of the rhythm of English. It takes a lot of practice to get used to such a rhythm. So, you need to start by identifying the stressed syllable in a word.

Listen for the strongly stressed words and phrases.

In English, key words and phrases that are essential to the meaning of a sentence are stressed louder. Therefore, pay attention to the words stressed with a higher pitch. When listening to an English recording for the first time, what matters most is to listen for a general understanding of what you hear. Do not try to hear every single word. Most of the unstressed words are articles or auxiliary verbs, which don't play an important role in the general context. At this level, you can ignore them.

Pay attention to liaisons.

In reading English, words are written with a space between them. There isn't such an obvious guide when it comes to listening to English. In oral English, there are many cases when the sounds of words are linked with adjacent words.

For instance, let's think about the phrase "**take off**," which can be used in "take off your clothes." "Take off your clothes" doesn't sound like [teɪk ɔːf] with each of the words completely and clearly separated from the others. Instead, it sounds as if almost all the words in context are slurred together, [ˈteɪkɔːf], for a more natural sound.

Shadow the voice of the native speaker.

Finally, you need to mimic the voice of the native speaker. Once you are sure you know how to pronounce all the words in a sentence, try to repeat them like an echo. Listen to the book again, but this time you should try a fun exercise while listening to the English.

This exercise is called "shadowing." The word "shadow" means a dark shade that is formed on a surface. When used as a verb, the word refers to the action of following someone or something like a shadow. In this exercise, pretend you are a parrot and try to shadow the voice of the native speaker.

Try to mimic the reader's voice by speaking at the same speed, with the same strong and weak stresses on words, and pausing or stopping at the same points.

Experts have already proven this technique to be effective. If you practice this shadowing exercise, your English speaking and listening skills will improve by leaps and bounds. While shadowing the native speaker, don't forget to pay attention to the meaning of each phrase and sentence.

Listen to what you want to shadow many times. Start out by just trying to shadow a few words or a sentence.

 Mimic the CD out loud. You can shadow everything the speaker says as if you are singing a round, or you also can speak simultaneously with the recorded voice of the native speaker.

 As you practice more, try to shadow more. For instance, shadow a whole sentence or paragraph instead of just a few words.

3 Listening Guide

以下為《清秀佳人》各章節的前半部。一開始若能聽清楚發音，之後就沒有聽力的負擔。先聽過摘錄的章節，之後再反覆聆聽括弧內單字的發音，並仔細閱讀各種發音的說明。

以下都是以英語的典型發音為基礎，所做的簡易說明，即使這裡未提到的發音，也可以配合音檔反覆聆聽，如此一來聽力必能更上層樓。

Chapter One page 14 🎧 34

Mathew Cuthbert was an (❶) (   ), almost (❷) years old. He and his sister, Marilla, lived at Green Gables. It (❸) (   ) small farm near the town of Avonlea.

❶ **old man:** old 和 man 連在一起唸時，old 的 [d] 音迅速略過，聽起來像是沒有發音。

❷ **sixty:** sixty (60) 和 sixteen (16) 常讓英語學習者分不清楚發音，其實 sixty 的重音在前，字尾的 [ti] 通常不太清楚。而 sixteen 的重音在後，[i:] 的發音會比較清楚，可以此做判斷。

❸ **was a:** was 的 -s 會和其後的 a 連在一起唸，聽起來就像是單獨一個字 wasa 的發音。

> The (❶) ( ) at breakfast, Marilla said, "Well, Anne, we have (❷) ( ) adopt you." Anne started to cry. "Why, child, what's the (❸)?" asked Marilla. "I'm crying," said Anne, "because I'm so happy! I (❹) ( ) here!

❶ **next morning:** next 的 -t 與 morning 一起發音時，[t] 會省略不發音，為美語發音的特徵。

❷ **decided to:** decided 的 -ed 發 [ɪd] 的音，但與 to 一起發音時，尾音 [d] 通常會略過不唸。而 to 除了在特別強調的時候以外，在日常生活中都會變化成 [tə] 的音。

❸ **matter:** 重音在第一音節，這個字的 t 位在兩個母音的中間，因此口語發音通常會將 t 發作 [d] 音。

❹ **love it:** love 和 it 連在一起唸時，love 的 [v] 音與 it 的 [ɪ] 音連音成為 [və] 的音。

> When school started in September, Anne and Diana
> (❶) ( ) school together. Diana said to Anne,
> "Today you'll meet Gilbert Blythe. He's very good-
> looking." "Oh, boys!" said Anne. "I'm not (❷)
> ( ) them."

❶ **walked to:** walked 原本的發音為 [wɔːkt]，但後面接 to 時與其 [t]
音連在一起只發一次音，因此需對照前後文來判斷時態。

❷ **interested in:** interested 的重音在第一個音節，其音標為
[ˋɪntrɪstɪd]，[d] 音會與 it 產生連音，成為 [dɪn] 的音。

Chapter Four page 54 🎧 37

> One day, Marilla (❶), "I'll ask the new vicar, Mr.
> Allan and his wife to my tea party on Wednesday."
> Anne was very excited. "Mrs. Allan is beautiful, and
> she has a very sweet smile! I'd like to make a (❷)
> ( ) ( ). Can I, please?"

❶ **announced:** 重音在第二音節，其音標為 [əˋnaʊnst]，最後一個音
[t] 會迅速略過，聽的時候需注意前後文來判斷動詞的時態。

❷ **cake for her:** cake 的尾音 [k] 會輕聲略過，幾乎聽不出來。

One day, (❶) told Anne that Miss Stacey. a new teacher, had come to Green Gables. "Anne, she thinks you are doing well in (❷). If you study well, you can pass the examination for Queen's College in Charottetown.

❶ **Marilla:** 重音在第二音節,相對來說在重音節周圍的發音聽起來會較微弱,所以這裡 ma 所發的音會聽不清楚,甚至被忽略而聽不出正確的發音。

❷ **school:** school 的 -c- 發有聲子音,通常 s 後面若緊接著 [p]、[t]、[k] 等音,就會出現接近沒有氣音的有聲子音。

Chapter Six page 80 🎧39

But when Anne arrived back at Green Gables, she felt something was wrong. Mathew looked much older than (❶). "What's the matter with him?" Anne asked Marilla. "He's had some heart problems (❷) (   )," replied Marilla.

❶ **before:** 重音在第二音節,整個字的正確發音為 [bɪˋfɚr],[bɪ] 音聽起來不明顯。

❷ **this year:** this 的尾音 [s] 會與 year 的發音 [jɪr] 成為連音 [sjɪr]。

4

Listening Comprehension

 A Listen to the CD and write down the answers.

Matthew	Diana	Gilbert	Stacey

❶ _____ ❷ _____ ❸ _____ ❹ _____

 B Listen to the CD and fill in the blanks.

❶ Anne was _____ the farm 'Green Gables.'
❷ Anne _____ to be a smart, independent woman.
❸ Mathew _____ a heart attack.

 C True or False.

T F ❶ ....

T F ❷ ....

🎧 43 **D** Match.

1 _____ •   • **a** so that she could help Marilla at Green Gables.

2 _____ •   • **b** even though he apologized to her several times.

3 _____ •   • **c** and turned her hair green.

4 _____ •   • **d** if he had not pulled her hair and said, 'carrots!'

🎧 44 **E** Listen to the CD and Choose the correct answer.

1 _____?

(a) A boy and an orphan girl who become friends.

(b) A little orphan girl who makes mistakes, but grows up well.

(c) A little girl's dream to become a teacher.

2 _____?

(a) Diana

(b) Marilla

(c) Gilbert

Translation

作者簡介　p. 4

露西・莫德・蒙哥馬利

（Lucy Maud Montgomery,
1874–1942）

　　露西・莫德・蒙哥馬利是加拿大的女作家，1874 年
11 月出生於一個叫愛德華王子島的小島。還是個小女孩的
她，便開始以寫作為樂。

　　1904 年，她讀著自己許久以前的日記，看見這行筆記：

　　「一對年邁夫妻向孤兒院申請領養一個男孩來幫忙農
場事務，在陰錯陽差下，卻送來個女孩。」

　　這引燃了她的想像，並啟發她創造出安妮（Anne）。

　　1905 年，《清秀佳人》（*Anne of Green Gables*）完成。
歷經十本安妮系列的著作，蒙哥馬利仍是個從日常取材的
作家，在她動人的描述下，美麗的風光景緻、溫馨情誼與
哀傷情懷躍然紙上。

《清秀佳人》的故事發生在加拿大，寧靜的艾凡里鎮（Avonlea）上的農場。馬修和瑪瑞拉是未婚的兄妹，住在農場裡。他們決定領養一個孤兒男孩來幫忙農事，然而孤兒院卻送來一個活潑健談的女孩。

自從這位叫安妮・雪麗的女孩，與開始他們同住在有著綠色屋頂的房子，每天都趣事不斷。安妮很介意自己的紅髮，同學吉伯特・布萊斯（Gilbert Blythe）的嘲笑讓兩人結成冤家，也讓安妮發奮用功唸書。

終於，安妮成功進入一所名聲響亮的大學。但因為馬修去世後，瑪瑞拉病情惡化，她放棄對學位的追求。吉伯特聽聞此事，辭去自己在艾凡里學校的教職，好讓安妮可以在那裡教書。最後，吉伯特和安妮也盡釋前嫌。

從 1908 年出版至今，安妮系列小說贏得了全球讀者的愛戴。

第一章　綠色小屋

p. 14–15 有一位年近六十歲的老爺爺，名叫馬修‧卡斯伯特，他和妹妹瑪瑞拉住在綠色小屋，那是在艾凡利鎮附近的一個小農場。

今天，馬修穿上他最體面的衣服，非常興奮，因為今天是個特別的日子。他駕車到艾凡利的火車站，詢問站長：「5 點 30 分的火車到了嗎？」

站長答道：「已經到了，有一位小女孩在等您，她就在那裡。」

馬修不敢置信地說：「一個小女孩？但我們要的是男孩！」

馬修和瑪瑞拉決定從孤兒院收養一位男孩，馬修需要人手幫忙農場上的工作。

馬修看到一位紅頭髮、纖瘦的小女孩，她看到馬修在注視著她，就跑過去，問道：

「您是綠色小屋的卡斯伯特先生嗎？」

p. 16–17 馬修還沒來得及回答，她繼續說：「很高興能夠認識您，聽到您要收養我，我真的很開心。」

馬修不知道該說什麼，他覺得對這小女孩很抱歉。馬修決定帶小女孩回家，他心想：「瑪瑞拉會告訴她，這件事情搞錯了。」

然而，在回家的路上，馬修很專注聽著安妮講話，她一路滔滔不絕！馬修不需要說任何話。

她說：「我的父母在我很小的時候就去世了，所以我一直都

很窮，一件好看的衣服也沒有。但是我會想像自己穿著漂亮的衣服，這樣我就會很開心！您偶爾也會想像一些東西嗎？」

馬修回答：「我……我……很少。」

小女孩問：「我的話應該不會太多吧？如果吵到您的話，請告訴我。」

馬修對她笑了笑，說：「妳繼續講，我喜歡聽妳說話。」

p. 18–19 他們到達綠色小屋時，瑪瑞拉到門口迎接，她笑著張開雙手。但是，當她看到小女孩時，她頓時收起笑臉：

「馬修，她是誰？」瑪瑞拉問，「男孩呢？」

馬修嘆了口氣說：「孤兒院弄錯了，他們送來的是女孩，而不是男孩。」

小女孩細聽之下，突然哭了起來，哭喊著：「你們不要我！你們要把我送回去了！」

瑪瑞拉拍著女孩的肩膀安慰她，「好，好，現在不要哭。」

女孩哭喊著：「這是我人生中最悽慘的事情了。」

瑪瑞拉對這女孩感到很抱歉，她說：「好吧，妳今晚可以在這裡住一晚。」

p. 20–21 「現在可以告訴我妳叫什麼名字嗎？」小女孩不哭了。「您可以叫我柯蒂莉亞嗎？」她問。

「柯蒂莉亞？那是妳的名字嗎？」

「不，不是，可是這名字很美，您不覺得嗎？」小女孩說：「我喜歡把我的名字想像是柯蒂莉亞，因為我真正的名字安妮・雪麗不好聽。」

瑪瑞拉搖搖頭，「這女孩的想像力也太豐富了吧。」她想。

當小女孩上床睡覺時，瑪瑞拉對馬修說道：「她明天必須回去孤兒院。」

　　馬修輕咳了幾聲，說：「瑪瑞拉，妳不覺得⋯⋯」他停了一下，「妳知道的，她是一個可愛的小人兒。」

　　瑪瑞拉叫道：「馬修·卡斯伯特！」她只有在生氣時才會連名帶姓一起叫他，「你是說你想要收養她嗎？」

p. 22–23 馬修感到不太自在，有一點緊張地說：「她很聰明，很有趣，又⋯⋯」

　　瑪瑞拉說：「但我們不需要女孩！她會很難照顧，而且對我們幫助不大。」

　　馬修回答說：「也許她需要我們。妳看，瑪瑞拉，她以前的生活一直都不快樂。她能幫妳做家事，我可以找村莊裡的男孩來幫忙做農活。妳覺得怎麼樣？」

　　瑪瑞拉想了很久，也實在為小女孩感到難過。最後，她說：「好吧，我同意，這個可憐的小女孩可以留下來，我會照顧她。」

　　馬修笑了笑，說：「瑪瑞拉，要好好對待她，我想她需要很多的愛。」

第二章　我喜歡這裡的生活

p. 26–27 隔天在吃早餐時，瑪瑞拉說：「這個嘛，安妮，我們決定收養妳了。」安妮哭了起來。

　　瑪瑞拉問：「怎麼了，孩子？」

　　安妮說：「我哭，是因為我太高興了！我喜歡這裡的生活，真是很謝謝您，謝謝！」

瑪瑞拉説：「不要哭了，孩子。」看到安妮哭，她心裡有點難過。

安妮不哭了，她説：「我可以叫您瑪瑞拉阿姨嗎？我一直都沒有家人，所以我好想要有一位和藹又仁慈的阿姨，我們可以想像一下您是我媽媽的姊妹。」

瑪瑞拉很驚訝，她堅定地回答道：「這不行。」

安妮聽了很詫異，問：「您從來都不曾想像過事情的嗎？」

瑪瑞拉答道：「我要做家事，要照顧馬修，在這裡我沒有時間去想像別的事情。」

p. 28-29 安妮沉默了一會兒，説：「瑪瑞拉，您想我在這裡會交到好朋友嗎？我一直都想要有好朋友。」

瑪瑞拉説：「我們的朋友具瑞，他們有個女兒，叫黛安娜，她十一歲，和妳一樣。」

安妮答道：「黛安娜！好美的名字啊！她的頭髮不是紅色的，對不對？希望不是。我討厭我的頭髮，紅色很醜。」

瑪瑞拉答道：「黛安納的頭髮是深色的。」

當安妮一看到黛安娜的時候，她們就知道彼此會成為好朋友。

早上的時候，安妮幫忙瑪瑞拉打掃房子，下午她去和黛安娜玩耍，或是當馬修先生在農場幹活時和他快樂地聊著天。

很快地，她就記住綠色小屋中每朵花、每棵樹、每隻動物的名字了，她喜歡這裡的每樣事物。

p. 30–31 有一位瑞秋・林德夫人，她喜歡探聽艾凡利的大小事情。她對卡斯伯特那孤兒院來的女孩很感興趣，林德夫人決定一訪綠色小屋。

瑪瑞拉迎接林德夫人走進農舍，告訴她所有關於安妮的事。

林德夫人說道：「所以妳和馬修決定要收養她了！」

瑪瑞拉微笑著說：「她是個聰明的小東西，她給這間屋子帶來了歡樂和笑聲。」

然而林德夫人卻難過地搖著頭：「妳錯了，瑪瑞拉。」

剛好這時安妮從花園跑進來，林德夫人看著這個纖瘦的小女孩，問道：「她很瘦，對吧？瑪瑞拉。看看那些小雀斑，還有那頭髮，紅得和胡蘿蔔一樣。」

安妮滿臉漲紅：「我討厭妳！」她生氣地叫喊：「我討厭妳！妳是個又胖又老又討厭的女人。」說完便跑回樓上的房間。

p. 32–33 「噢，真可怕的小孩！」林德夫人說。「我可以告訴妳，有這個小女孩，妳會惹來很多麻煩！」

瑪瑞拉回答：「妳會對她不是很尊重，瑞秋。」

林德夫人很驚訝：「好吧！我想這個孤兒院來的女孩對妳來說，比我還要重要。我真替妳感到可憐，就這樣吧，再見。」

之後，瑪瑞拉上樓走到安妮的房間。那孩子躺在她窄小的床上，臉靠在枕頭上哭泣。

瑪瑞拉溫柔地說：「妳不該那樣發脾氣的。」

安妮抬起頭說：「她對我很不好。」

瑪瑞拉說：「我懂妳的感受，但是妳必須為妳的失禮向她道歉才行。」

安妮低下頭，「我才不要呢。」她說。

瑪瑞拉板起臉說：「那妳就必須待在房間好好想一想，等妳準備好要道歉的時候才能出來。」

p. 34-35 沒有安妮，早午晚餐的時刻都變得很安靜。

　　這天晚上，馬修默默地上樓，小女孩難過地坐在窗戶旁。馬修說：「安妮，為什麼不道歉呢？」

　　安妮說：「很抱歉，我昨天太過生氣了，但是當我早上醒來時，我一點都不氣了，甚至覺得有點難為情。但是，你們真的要我……道歉嗎？」

　　馬修說：「沒錯，我們希望如此。」

　　她說：「我真的不想向那個女人道歉，」她看著馬修仁慈的臉孔，「但是我願意為你們做任何事。」

　　她嘆了口氣說：「好吧，我去道歉。」

　　馬修露出笑容：「這樣才是好女孩！」

p. 36-37 瑪瑞拉很高興聽到安妮願意道歉了。稍晚時，她和安妮去拜訪林德夫人。安妮在林德夫人暖和的廚房中跪下。

　　「哦，林德夫人，」小女孩哭著說，「我很抱歉。我無法表達我有多抱歉，但您一定可以想像。請您原諒我，假如您不原諒我，我一輩子都會很難過的。」

　　瑪瑞拉仔細觀察安妮，她覺得安妮不是真心感到抱歉。然而，林德夫人仁慈地說：

　　「安妮，我當然會原諒你。我說妳的頭髮紅得很可怕，但別擔心，我有個朋友以前也像妳的頭髮一樣紅，但是她長大就變成了美麗的褐色。現在，妳可以去我的花園玩耍了。」

　　安妮走了之後，林德夫人轉向瑪瑞拉：「她是個奇怪的小女孩，很容易生氣，也能很快冷靜下來。一個小孩子最好能隱藏自己的情緒。她的說話方式很奇怪，但我喜歡她。」

第三章　我討厭你，吉伯特

p. 40–41 九月分學期開始時，安妮和黛安娜在校園內並肩同行，黛安娜對安妮說：「今天妳會看到吉伯特‧布萊斯，他很帥喔。」

安妮說：「噢，男生啊，我對他們沒興趣！」

然而當她在校園裡看到吉伯特時，卻仔細地瞧了瞧他。他個子高高的，有著一頭棕色的鬈髮，笑容可掬。

她小聲地告訴黛安娜說：「他長得超帥的耶。」

隔天，艾凡利校園很安靜，菲利浦老師在教室後面，幫忙指導一些年紀較大的學生。安妮則望著窗外，做著白日夢。

吉伯特看到安妮，要和她說說話。他小聲地說：「嗨，安妮！」

安妮沒有聽到吉伯特在叫她，她正想像自己在美麗的樹上乘風飛翔。

吉伯特很意外，通常女孩們都很願意和他說話的。

p. 42–43 他伸出手拉了拉安妮的頭髮，喊著：「紅蘿蔔，紅蘿蔔！」

安妮跳了起來，她看著吉伯特，「真糟糕的男生！」她喊叫著：「我討厭你！」接著就拿起書本往他頭上打下去！

菲利浦先生看到安妮用書本打吉伯特的頭，便說道：「安妮，妳怎麼這樣呢？」

吉伯特大聲地說：「菲利浦先生，都是我的錯，我對她太沒禮貌了，她才會打我。」

菲利浦先生對安妮的作為不高興，他說：「無論如何都不能打同學。安妮，上去站在教室前面。」

安妮整個下午都站在教室前面，她看起來很生氣。「我討厭菲利浦先生，」她想：「我也討厭吉伯特‧布萊斯，我再也不要和他說話了！」

p. 44-45 隔天，有些男同學午餐時間在操場玩耍，下午上課時遲到，安妮和他們一起跑進教室，剛好在菲利浦先生後面。

菲利浦先生說：「妳遲到了，妳今天不能和黛安娜坐，我看妳很喜歡和男孩子在一起，所以妳今天下午就坐在吉伯特旁邊。」

她想：「他不是說真的吧！」不過菲利浦先生倒是很認真，他說：「妳聽到了嗎，安妮？」

安妮輕聲回答：「好的，老師。」

她收拾書本，慢慢搬到吉伯特旁的座位，然後坐下，把頭趴在桌上。

她心想：「又不是只有我遲到，為什麼菲利浦先生要讓我和男生坐在一起？而且還是和最差勁的男生吉伯特‧布萊斯坐在一起！」

那天下午，對珍妮來說真是好漫長。

p. 46–47 放學後，安妮搬回去她的座位，收拾書本、筆和鉛筆。

黛安娜問：「妳在做什麼？」

安妮說：「我不要再來學校了」

黛安娜說：「噢，不要啦，安妮，我們要讀一本新書耶！星期一要玩遊戲，會很刺激的！」但是安妮不在乎。

那天晚上，瑪瑞拉去拜訪林德夫人：「瑞秋，給我一些忠告吧！安妮說她再也不要回去學校上課了！我應該要怎麼勸她啊？」

當然，林德夫人已經知道安妮在學校惹的麻煩。

林德夫人說：「這個嘛，瑪瑞拉，我自己養了十個小孩，所以我可以告訴妳，不要擔心，讓安妮好好想一想，她很快就會想要回去學校的。」

於是瑪瑞拉什麼也沒做，而安妮也就待在家裡沒去學校。

p. 48–49 有一天，瑪瑞拉發現安妮在哭，讓她嚇了一跳。她問道：「怎麼了，孩子？」

安妮啜泣著說：「我好想念黛安娜，我不能沒有她，瑪瑞拉。她要是結婚了，我怎麼辦？我已經開始討厭她以後的老公了！我可以想像她在教堂穿著白紗的樣子，那時她就要離開我了！我就永遠不能見到她了！」

瑪瑞拉忍住不笑出來，但她忍俊不禁。安妮抬起頭盯著瑪瑞拉，突然覺得自己很蠢。

隔天，安妮回到了學校，所有孩子都很高興再看到她，尤其是戴安娜。然而，安妮沒跟吉伯特·布萊斯講話，她還很氣他，她想她永遠都不會原諒他了。

第四章　安妮的錯誤

p. 54-55 有一天，瑪瑞拉宣佈：「我曾邀請新牧師，艾倫先生，以及他的夫人來參加星期三的茶點派對。」

安妮聽了很興奮。「艾倫夫人長得很美，而且笑容可掬，我想為她做一塊蛋糕，可以嗎？」

瑪瑞拉說：「好呀，妳可以為她做一塊蛋糕。」

星期三終於到來，每個人都圍坐喝著茶，瑪瑞拉做了很多小蛋糕，配上安妮做的特製蛋糕。

艾倫夫人說：「這些蛋糕很好吃，卡斯伯特女士。」

瑪瑞拉說：「這是我的榮幸，但蛋糕不全是我做的。這一個，妳吃吃看，這是安妮特別為妳做的。」

艾倫夫人拿起蛋糕吃了一點。突然間，她的表情變得怪怪的。

瑪瑞拉問：「有什麼事不對勁嗎？」她很快地也吃了一塊安妮的蛋糕，然後說道：

「噢，安妮！妳放了什麼在蛋糕裡面？」安妮滿臉通紅。

p. 56-57 安妮問：「怎麼了？妳不喜歡嗎？」

瑪瑞拉說：「喜歡？很難吃耶！艾倫夫人，別吃了。安妮，妳把我的藥放進蛋糕裡了！」

安妮答道：「哦，我不知道那是藥啊，它白白的，放在瓶子裡，我以為那是牛奶！」安妮感到眼淚湧了上來，她跑到樓上的床上。

她沒有下樓來和艾倫夫婦道別。

每個人都離開後，瑪瑞拉上樓來到安妮的房間。

安妮哭著說：「瑪瑞拉，我很丟臉！」

瑪瑞拉對她笑了笑，拭去她臉上的淚珠。

「艾倫夫人沒有生氣，她還說妳特別為她做了蛋糕，真是太貼心了！」瑪瑞拉說。

安妮停止哭泣，問道：「她原諒我了嗎？她人真的是太好了。」

她皺著眉頭，說道：「我為什麼老是犯這種錯誤？」

瑪瑞拉笑著說：「噢，妳還會犯更多的錯的，妳很擅長犯錯的呀！」

p. 58 四月的一個晚上，瑪瑞拉拜訪完朋友回到家已經很晚了。她上樓去看安妮。

安妮哭著說：「不要盯著我看，瑪瑞拉！我知道我看起來很糟，我知道！」

瑪瑞拉問：「怎麼了？」

安妮哭著說：「瑪瑞拉，我不想活了！您看我的頭髮！」

瑪瑞拉看到安妮的紅髮變成了可怕的深綠色。瑪瑞拉提高嗓門說：「安妮，妳做了什麼？」

安妮忍著不哭，解釋說：「我跟一個來敲門的男子買了一罐東西，他說那個可以把我的紅髮變成黑色的！噢，我真蠢，竟然會相信他！」

p. 60-61 瑪瑞拉反覆地洗安妮的頭髮，但髮色還是綠色的。安妮在家裡待了整整一星期，除了瑪瑞拉和馬修，她誰也不見。

週末時，瑪瑞拉終於說：「安妮，我很抱歉，但妳不能一直待在家，可是也不能留著一頭綠髮去上課，我們要把它全部給剪掉。」

安妮難過地說道：「我想您是對的，或許這教會了我不要妄想會變美麗。」

隔天在學校，看到安妮的頭髮剪得這麼短，每個人都很吃驚。他們問安妮發生了什麼事，但是安妮一個字也沒說。

　　幾個禮拜後，安妮開始長出一些新髮，是比較深色的紅色捲髮，安妮感到很高興。

　　p. 62-63 那個夏天，安妮和朋友到河邊嬉戲，她們發現那裡有一艘舊船。安妮有個主意。

　　「我來想像我是一個囚犯，我要乘船逃獄。」安妮告訴朋友們：「我會躲在船裡，河水會把船帶到橋那一邊。你們假裝是我的家人，在橋邊等我。」

　　其他女孩都表同意，所以安妮就上了船，然後他們把船推到河裡。

　　安妮要扮演囚犯，覺得很興奮。然而，她突然覺得濕濕的，船的底部有水滲進來了！水一直湧進船內，眼看船就要沉了！

　　安妮急忙四處張望，她看到河邊有幾棵樹，便跳上樹，抓著樹枝。

　　安妮的朋友在橋邊等，卻看到船到漂到角落，沉了下去。

　　她們很害怕，因為沒有看到安妮。他們大叫：「安妮溺水了！」女孩們跑到村裡去尋求幫助。

　　p. 64-65 可憐的安妮遇上了麻煩，她雙手掛在河上方的樹枝上。

　　突然，她聽見一個熟悉的聲音：「我抓到妳了！」安妮看到吉伯特‧布萊斯坐在他自己的船上。他動作迅速地幫忙安妮上了他的船。

她冷冷地說一聲：「謝謝你！」

他很快說道：「安妮，我很抱歉，曾經叫妳『紅蘿蔔』。那是很久以前的事了，我覺得妳現在的頭髮很好看，我們把以前的事忘記，當好朋友好嗎？」

有這麼一時，安妮想要答應，但她突然記起了曾因吉伯特，害她在教室前罰站的事。

她冷冷地回答：「不，吉伯特·布萊斯，我永遠都不會當你的朋友。」

吉伯特生氣地說：「那好吧！安妮·雪麗，我再也不會請妳和我做朋友了！」

安妮帶著傲氣走回家，內心裡卻感到一股莫名的悲傷，很想哭。

第五章　妳做到了！

p. 68–69 有一天，瑪瑞拉告訴安妮，新來的老師史黛希小姐來過綠色小屋。

瑪瑞拉說道：「安妮，她覺得妳在學校表現良好，假如妳認真唸書，通過夏洛特鎮女王大學的考試，等大學唸完一年，妳就可以成為老師！」

安妮聽了很高興，說：「噢，我喜歡當老師！」

於是之後的下午時間，安妮會和一些同學留在學校待到很晚，史黛希小姐會幫他們準備考試。

黛安娜不想去上女王大學，所以她很早就回家了，但吉伯特也和安妮一起都留在學校裡。他們兩個人互相都不說話。

每個人都知道他們是死對頭，他們兩個都想要考最高分。但其實，安妮心裡想和吉伯特成為朋友，只是現在已經太遲了。

p. 70 有一天，林德夫人去拜訪瑪瑞拉，林德夫人説：「妳的安妮現在是一個大女孩了，她都比妳還高了！」

瑪瑞拉説：「妳説得沒錯，端秋。」

林德夫人説：「她確實已經出落得亭亭玉立了！妳看那對美麗的灰色眼睛，還有紅棕色的頭髮！妳把她照顧得很好。」

瑪瑞拉説：「謝謝妳。」瑪瑞拉很高興，也很驕傲。

過後，那大晚上，馬修發現瑪瑞拉在廚房偷偷哭泣。

馬修問道：「瑪瑞拉，怎麼了？」

瑪瑞拉答道：「沒事，我只是想到安妮離我們而去時，我會很想她。」

馬修很驚訝：「妳是説她去上大學的時候？別難過，瑪瑞拉，她週末和假日都會回來的。」

瑪瑞拉傷心地説：「我還是會想她。」

p. 72–73 時間過得很快，在六月初的一個溫暖夏日，安妮前往應試。

那天下午，安妮回到綠色小屋，她仍然很緊張。

「噢，我希望我考得不錯，考題很難！我要等三個星期才知道結果。」她説。

黛安娜第一個知道了消息。她跑去綠色小屋的廚房，揮舞著報紙，大聲嚷道：「看，安妮，妳的名字排在第一個！還有吉伯特也考過了！」

安妮用顫掉的雙手接過報紙，看到她的名字排在二百名學生中的第一位。

她這輩子第一次説不出話來。馬修帶著溫暖的笑容説：「好，妳看，我就知道妳一定能辦到的。」

瑪瑞拉説：「安妮，做得好。」他們都很高興。

p. 74 之後連續三個禮拜，安妮和瑪瑞拉都很忙，安妮需要新衣服去上學。

在她離家前一晚，安妮穿上一件洋裝給馬修看，瑪瑞拉也在一旁看著。瑪瑞拉想起五年前那個常犯錯的瘦小女孩，便哭了起來。

安妮問道：「您怎麼哭了？」

瑪瑞拉答道：「我只是想起妳還是小女孩的樣子，而現在，妳要走了，沒有妳在身邊，我……我……我會很孤單的。」

安妮握著瑪瑞拉的手，說道：「瑪瑞拉，一切都不會變的，我可能會愈長愈高大，年紀也愈來愈大，但我會一直是您的小安妮，而且我也會一天比一天更愛您和馬修，還有綠色小屋的。」

p. 76-77 隔年，安妮住在夏洛特鎮，每天都去大學上課。吉伯特也上女王大學，安妮有時會看到他。然而，她不願意主動先和他說話，而吉伯特也從不瞧她一眼。

接近年終時有幾個考試。「我要得最高分，」她想，「說不定我還可以獲得艾佛瑞獎呢。」

艾佛瑞獎是頒給文章寫得最棒的學生。她想要得到艾佛瑞獎，因為贏得艾佛瑞獎的學生會獲得在瑞德蒙德大學就讀四年的獎學金。這所大學是加拿大其中一間最好的學校。

這天，考試結果公布，安妮不敢親自去看榜。然而，她聽到朋友喊道：「是吉伯特，他考最高分。」安妮聽了很不開心。

不久，她又聽到了自己的名字，「安妮獲得了艾佛瑞獎！」全部朋友都圍著她，雀躍歡呼。安妮心想，「馬修和瑪瑞拉一定會很高興的。」

第六章　馬修和瑪瑞拉

p. 80–81 然而，當安妮回到綠色小
屋時，她卻覺得有些事不對勁。馬
修看起來比以前老多了。

安妮問瑪瑞拉：「他怎麼了？」

瑪瑞拉答道：「他今年心臟有一些毛病。」

安妮說：「您看起來也不好。」

「我的頭常常會痛，就在眼睛後面。」瑪瑞拉停了一會
兒，又說：「還有一件事，妳有聽到有關教會銀行的事嗎？」

安妮答道：「我聽說它有些問題。」

瑪瑞拉說：「是啊，我們的錢都在那個銀行裡，我知道
馬修很擔心。」

隔天，馬修收到一封信，他打開信，臉色大變。

瑪瑞拉高聲說：「怎麼了？」安妮也盯著馬修的臉看。

突然間，馬修倒在地上。安妮和瑪瑞拉試著要喚醒馬修，
但是太遲了，馬修已經死了。

p. 82 醫生來的時候說：「是他心臟的問題，他最近有聽
到什麼壞消息嗎？」

「是信！」安妮喊道：「我們來看看，噢，瑪瑞拉，您看！
教會銀行關閉了，所有銀行客戶的錢都拿不回來了！您的和
馬修的錢都沒有了！」

艾凡利的每個人聽到馬修去世的消
息，都感到很難過。剛開始，安妮沒有哭，
後來她想到馬修聽到她得到艾佛瑞獎時的
笑容，就突然哭得無法停止。

瑪瑞拉抱著她，兩人一起啜泣著。

瑪瑞拉小聲説：「哭也不能讓他回來了，安妮，我們必須學會過沒有馬修的生活。」

　　p. 84　幾天後，瑪瑞拉説：「安妮，等妳去瑞德蒙德大學時，我會想妳的。艾凡利的其他學生有什麼打算嗎？」

　　安妮答道：「有些人要教書，有些人會繼續念王后大學。」

　　瑪瑞拉問：「那吉伯特呢？他不是要去艾凡利的學校教書嗎？」

　　安妮沒回答。瑪瑞拉繼續説：「他現在又高又英俊，妳不覺得他像他爸爸約翰嗎？妳也知道，很多年前約翰和我是很好的朋友。」

　　安妮很驚訝：「發生了什麼事？你們為什麼沒有……」

　　瑪瑞拉説：「嗯，我們以前吵過架，我忘記是為了什麼事，他希望我們重新和好，但是我無法原諒他。我之後很後悔，但他不再跟我説話了。假如我們……，噢，算了，那是很久以前的事了。」

　　p. 86　隔天，瑪瑞拉去了醫院，回來時一臉倦容。安妮問道：「醫生怎麼説呢？」

　　「假如不小心照顧，我半年內就會失明！」

　　安妮震驚得説不出話來。瑪瑞拉説：「不用擔心我，我想我會賣掉農場。」瑪瑞拉哭了起來。

　　那天晚上，安妮坐在床旁，她想了很久。在上床前，她心裡有了一個計畫。

　　隔天早上，安妮告訴瑪瑞拉她的計畫：

　　「您不能賣掉綠色小屋，這是我們的家！您聽聽看，我有個很棒的主意，我不會去念瑞德蒙德大學，那裡太遠了。我會去附近村莊的學校教書。這樣我平時就可以住那裡，週末再回家來幫忙。這個計畫不錯吧？」

p. 88–89 「噢，安妮，」瑪瑞拉說：「如果妳能待在這裡，那麼一切都可以解決了。但是妳想去唸書的話，就一定要去瑞德蒙德大學。」

安妮笑著說：「瑞德蒙德不重要，我會是一個很棒的老師，這是我能做到最好的事了。」

瑪瑞拉搖搖頭，忍著眼淚：「安妮，妳真是一個好女孩。」

幾天之後，林德夫人來拜訪他們，她帶來一些好消息，「妳們知道吉伯特決定離職了嗎？」

安妮問：「為什麼？」

林德夫人說：「當他聽到妳的計畫時，他便決定離職，這樣一來，妳就可以在艾凡利當老師，住在綠色小屋了。」

安妮很驚訝：「噢，他人真好！」

p. 90–91 那天稍晚時，安妮在河邊散步，她看見吉伯特。

安妮停下來向他揮手，她輕聲說：「吉伯特，你做的事真的太令人窩心了，很謝謝你！」

吉伯特說：「安妮，我很高興能夠幫到妳，我們現在是好朋友了嗎？妳已經原諒我叫妳『紅蘿蔔』了嗎？」

安妮噗哧一笑，「我早就原諒你了，」她說，「我想我們會是很好的朋友。」

吉伯特說：「我能和妳一起散步回家嗎？」

當安妮回到綠色小屋的廚房時，瑪瑞拉說：「安妮，妳看起來很高興。和妳一起回來的人是吉伯特嗎？」

「是的，瑪瑞拉。」安妮回答，滿臉通紅。

「吉伯特和我決定要當好朋友，噢，瑪瑞拉，我想我們都會過得很幸福的，我們有彼此，而且我們擁有綠色小屋，夫復何求啊？」

Answers

P. 24　A　① thin　② red　③ imagination

　　　B　① F　② T　③ T　④ F

P. 25　C　① did want　② does like

　　　D　① adopt　② made　③ sent　④ enjoyed
　　　　　⑤ decided

P. 38　A　① upset　② ashamed　③ pleased

　　　B　① (b)　② (c)

P. 39　C　① F　② T　③ F

　　　D　① What a tall tree　② What a pretty doll
　　　　　③ What a nice girl

P. 50　A　① in, in　② up, up　③ at, at

　　　B　① friendly　② horrible　③ exciting　④ serious

P. 51　C　① pulled, carrots　② sit next to　③ advice

　　　D　① F　② T　③ T

P. 66　A　① vicar　② tears　③ prisoner　④ drowned

　　　B　④ → ⑤ → ① → ② → ③

P. 67　C　① (b)　② (a)

(D) **1** (c)

P. 78　(A)　**1** however　**2** before　**3** because

(B)　**1** -(c)　**2** -(d)　**3** -(b)　**4** -(a)

P. 79　(C)　**1** (b)　**2** (b)

(D)　**1** F　**2** F　**3** T

P. 92　(A)　**1** (b)　**2** (c)

(B)　**1** T　**2** T　**3** F

P. 106　(A)　**1** Anne's best childhood friend.　— **Diana**
　　　　　2 A quiet, shy man who likes to listen to
　　　　　Anne's stories.　— **Matthew**
　　　　　3 A teacher that helps Anne study for college.
　　　　　— **Stacey**
　　　　　4 A boy that Anne hates when she is a child.
　　　　　— **Gilbert**

(B)　**1** raised on　**2** grew up　**3** died of

(C)　**1** Anne studied at Queen's College.　(T)
　　　2 Gilbert saved Anne from the river.　(T)

P. 107　(D)　**1** Anne decided not to go to Redmond – (a)
　　　　　2 Anne would not forgive Gilbert – (b)
　　　　　3 Anne might have liked Gilbert – (d)
　　　　　4 Anne bought some hair dye – (c)

(E)　**1** What is the main idea of the story?　(b)
　　　2 At school and at college, whom is Anne mainly
　　　competing against for high scores?　(c)

Adaptor of *Anne of Green Gables*

Brian J. Stuart

University of Utah (Mass communication/Journalism)
Sookmyung Women's University, English Instructor

清秀佳人【二版】
Anne of Green Gables

作者 _ 露西‧莫德‧蒙哥馬利
　　　　（Lucy Maud Montgomery）

改寫 _ Brian J. Stuart

插圖 _ An Ji-yeon

翻譯 / 編輯 _ 劉心怡

作者 / 故事簡介翻譯 _ 王采翎

校對 _ 張盛傑

封面設計 _ 林書玉

排版 _ 葳豐／林書玉

播音員 _ Kate Ferguson, Michael Yancey

製程管理 _ 洪巧玲

發行人 _ 周均亮

出版者 _ 寂天文化事業股份有限公司

電話 _ +886-2-2365-9739

傳真 _ +886-2-2365-9835

網址 _ www.icosmos.com.tw

讀者服務 _ onlineservice@icosmos.com.tw

出版日期 _ 2020年2月 二版一刷（250201）

郵撥帳號 _ 1998620-0 寂天文化事業股份有限公司

國家圖書館出版品預行編目資料

清秀佳人 / Lucy Maud Montgomery 原著 ; Brian J.
Stuart 改寫 . -- 二版 . -- 臺北市 : 寂天文化, 2020.02
　　面；　　公分
譯自 : Anne of green gables

ISBN 978-986-318-894-0(25K 平裝附光碟片)
885.357　　　　　　　　　　　　　　　109000890